Violence and Drugs Only
By T. Marie & DAK

D1519259

Dedication

To my Ley and Aziz, our life has changed tremendously and it's all for a good cause. You help keep me whole, sane, and alive. We are on a new journey and mommy is so excited for it. Good things come to those who wait and it's only up from here now. In this book we express the dynamic between a family. Proving that siblings don't always get along, or aren't always right. You ain't gotta like your brother or sister. But you'll always love them. And I love y'all, y'all are my reason. I'm not gonna stop grinding and making the impossible possible. Cause no matter what, I got y'all. Just always have each other too.

To Tiff, thank you for the collab. Literally writing until the day you gave birth. If that's not determination, I don't know what is. Super proud of you and once again. Congrats on Baby Trent Money. Welcome to motherhood friend.

- DAK aka Mommy

Daddy Joseph Singleton- You left me in this cruel world on 10/25/18. I love you with everything in my and I will forever miss you. Everything you taught me I will live by it. Everything I do I'm doing it for you and Terry. You're my angel now and I will always remember your last words to me and it will forever be engraved in my heart (I love you to baby.) When I feel like giving up I know I can always look in the sky and know you're watching over me. When I want to break down and cry I know you will forever comfort me even though you're not her physically. You have your wings now daddy. I miss you much, but I have to try to keep living, even though its hard I know you'll whoop my tail if I gave up. Rest peacefully daddy. -Your baby girl.

Goddaddy Terry Underwood-
May 24, 2009 you left me and I vowed to always make you proud. I know since then I have done nothing but make you smile in heaven. I know you and daddy living up. You have your best friend back with you now. Just know that I will always make you both proud. Rest peacefully goddaddy-

I would also like to give a special thanks to my cousins Tanya and Vern Boone and my Uncle Jerry. I love y'all watch over me. .

I would like to give a special thanks to my mother Ethel Burnett When others doubted me you to pushed me to be the best I could be, and I will forever be grateful for that. To my sisters Sha'Mara Scales and Callie Russell, thank you for being my role models and helping me set goals and achieving them all. A girl couldn't ask for a better support system. To my readers, thank you all for your support. I wouldn't be who I am without either of you. I love bringing you books that has you on the edge of your seating and scratching you heads.

To my baby boy Trenton mommy love you with everything in her! Everything I'm doing is for you. I love you all and always remember to keep striving for the best and reaching for the stars.

To Dak, thank you so much for joining this journey for me! I couldn't have did it without you!

- Tiffany Singleton

Chapter 1

"Yo, make some muthafucking noise if you enjoying yoself at the Summer Jam today." DJ Wreck yelled over Megan Thee Stallion's newest song *Body*. Carson "Sonny" Vado, the youngest of the Vado brothers, walked around with a cup to his lips taking sips of Hennessy. He was at the best concert of the summer. Everybody and their mothers were outside and just having a good time. Food, drinks, music, and gas filled the air. The blunt and Henny combo had Sonny lit.

"Yo bro look at all these big booty bitches. I'm taking one of these hoes to a hotel and dropping nothing but dick in her tonight. Shit, I might take two of these bitches with me." Sonny laughed over the music as he spoke to his brother Denetro, better known as Nitro. Nitro laughed and shook his head knowing his brother was drunk and it wasn't even six, but shit, it was six somewhere.

"Sonny, calm yo ass down." Akiel whispered in his ear while throwing his arm over his baby brother's shoulder. He took the cup of Henny from Sonny's hand knowing he'd had enough. Sonny was hotheaded and he was just trying to enjoy his day without any problems.

"I'm good Kill. Y'all forgetting I'm a grown ass man."

"A grown ass man no haffi say him a grown ass man." Kill's patois revealed itself out of anger as he spoke to Carson. He walked off with Sonny's blunt and cup needing him to sober up a little bit. He was giving Sonny his space knowing that he had a spiraling temper, and today he just didn't have time for it. He'd came out to enjoy himself and as he watched Sonny's dreads covering his face Kill knew Sonny's anger was gonna get them put out. It wouldn't have been the first time. He knew his brother well enough, and he could feel the bullshit permeating off of Sonny.

Kill shook his head as Sonny poured himself another drink. He headed towards him again. "A drunk do whateva widout thinking of di consequences baby bro." He warned, knowing it was time for Sonny to put the drink down. Kill only spoke patois when his anger was taking over him. Sonny smirked at him while taking another sip of his drink. He didn't listen to his brothers and he wasn't about to start now.

The three brothers walked around, mingling a little as Kill and Nitro made sure they watched over Sonny since he hadn't put his cup down. Sloppy wasn't how they moved but they knew once Sonny started his shit, there was no stopping his ass. The only thing they could do was watch him and have his back.

"Kill, when you gone let me ride you like a bike." A woman with a watermelon sized ass walked up to him, damn near pushing her titties on him.

"Mi nuh fuck wid whores mama, ave sum class a maybe you can get di dick." Nitro spit up his liquor and held his stomach laughing at Kill. The woman had caught him at a bad time and he didn't have any patience to play nice. She walked away with embarrassment etched on her face.

"You didn't have to do her like that bro." Nitro told him while shaking his head. Kill waved him off, as he continued to make his rounds around the arena as Lil Baby performed on the stage. Everyone rapped his song word for word like they'd helped him write it.

Kill grabbed Sonny, stopping him from beating the man up. They watched as someone helped the guy off the ground. He lunged towards Sonny once he regained balance and the man who picked him up grabbed him.

"Negro sabes quiné soy!" (Nigga you know who the fuck I am) The drunk man barked at Sonny. He was trying his hardest to get to him but his friend wouldn't let him go.

"Calm yo guy down and I'll calm my brother down. We just trying to have a good time." Kill told the man as he pushed Sonny towards Nitro, only pissing Sonny off more.

"Get the fuck off me. I'm not some little ass nigga."

Nitro grabbed the back of Sonny's neck. "Chill lil bro lets take a walk baby. Look at all the bad bitches in attendance." He tried to swindle him as he led Sonny away from the other man.

"I'll see you around bitch ass nigga. Run up on me and imma fuck you up." Sonny yelled making a scene.

"Stare in the mirror whenever you drive, Overprotecti

crazy for mine, you gotta pay attention to the signs, Seem lik

blind following the blind, Thinking 'bout everything that's g

I boost security up at my home, I'm with my kind if they rig

they wrong" Sonny rapped in Kill's face showing him he w

a good time. He was rubbing his arrogance in his brother's

Akiel struggled to have fun. He was always on guard and

wanted him to let his dreads down.

The Vado brothers was the most notorious Jamai

Georgia. Every nigga wanted to be them and every bitch

fuck them. They got nothing but respect as they walked

arena. It wasn't common for them to be outside when it

business. So they took advantage of the day they were

"Aye man watch where the fuck you going." S

drunk Mexican man who'd accidentally stepped on hi

and red Jordan 2 Retro. The brown drink in the man's

onto the ground adding color onto Sonny's shoes. "N

wasted yo cheap ass drink on my new fucking J's."

he pushed the man harder this time causing him to s

"Yo man, excuse my hotheaded brother." Kill told the Mexicans. Mugs were on all their faces. They were looking like they were ready for any kind of smoke coming their way. Shaking his head, Kill went to find his brothers because he knew some shit was gone pop off before the end of the day.

"Mi tell you nuh fi start no bullshit and yuh go and start bullshit. Wi nuh need any unnecessary beef, di fuck you thinking." Kill was in Sonny's face grilling him before Sonny pushed him back. Kill pulled his pants up ready to charge at Sonny until Nitro stepped between them.

"We don't beef with each other in public bro, handle him in private and have his back in public you know that." Nitro reminded Kill of the law they'd created as he kept eye contact.

"Let's get the fuck out of here because shit is gonna pop off cause of that lil nigga." Taking the lead, Kill walked towards the exit, making sure that their shooters were still in place.

"Nigga, I'm not leaving yet. When have we ever let some niggas run us out of somewhere. I'm not going nowhere, imma finish enjoying myself." Sonny walked the opposite way from Kill, and headed towards the bar so he could refill his cup. Sonny was confident. He had his bitch on his hip and wouldn't hesitate to drop bodies.

"You know the vibes Akiel, we move as one. If he stays, we stay." Nitro added walking away from Kill. As much as he wanted to leave, he couldn't leave them behind. Nitro and Sonny were like Frick and Frack. They were close in age and Nitro had a soft spot for Sonny that he didn't have for anyone else. His intermittent explosive disorder allowed Nitro to be his voice of reasoning whenever Sonny was unable to use his words. Sonny's short temper had put them in worst scenarios. Nitro's goal was to diffuse situations before shit got out of control.

Against his better judgement Kill met them at the bar. He needed a drink but wasn't going to indulge anymore because he refused to bury his brothers. They were both drunk as fuck. And their guards were too low for Kill's liking.

"Yo we got the hottest female rapper out right now about to perform for us. Let's show some love for Megan Thee Stallion." As soon as DJ Wreck announced her presence the crowd went crazy and they made their way to the front of the stage.

look at how I bodied that, ate it up and gave it back

Yeah, you look good, but they still wanna know where Megan at

All the women went crazy when she started rapping. There was ass twerking everywhere and it was a fucking sight to see. Sonny stood behind one of the girls placing his hard dick print behind her ass. When she saw who it was she began popping her ass a little harder trying to be the woman he took home for the night. If there was one thing everyone could agree on about Sonny, it was he didn't give no fucks and the bullshit that happened earlier was the last thing on his mind. He was easily set off, easily calmed down when he no longer felt pressure. The only thing he was worried about was getting his dick wet tonight and giving a bitch some good ass Henny dick.

When he looked to his left, he seen the nigga who wasted his drink on his shoes coming towards him. He didn't hesitate to lift his shirt, showing his gun and the dude stopped instantly. Laughing to himself, Sonny grabbed the girl by her waist and grinded into her. "You going with me tonight. Put yo number in my phone." He said in her ear while handing her his phone. She followed his direction and Sonny didn't hesitate to save it under *Summer jam hoe.* "I'll text you where to meet me, come with yo throat relaxed." He joked while walking away from her. He was a rude muthafucka but bitches loved him.

Once everything began to die down hours later, Kill let his brothers know it was time to go before it was too hard to get out. Kill felt the vibe in the air and wasn't trying to chance anything. They'd already stayed too long for his liking. The minute they made it outside the gate, Kill took note of the Mexicans he'd spotted. He stopped in his tracks giving his brothers a look as his hand fell over the gun on his hip.

stantly the sharp shooter on the roof began tagging every Mexican

th red dots, dropping each one in sight. As the bodies dropped.

ll stood from behind the car he was taking cover behind and

rted shooting with guns in both hands. "Yuh niggas think wi sum

ch niggas or someting! Wi run Georgia, dis mi muthafucking city

y." Kill was shooting and hitting anyone he could.

POW POW POW POW

Sonny and Nitro joined their brother both standing beside

. It was then the Mexican's realized that although they rode deep,

Vado brother's rode smart. A sharp shooter at any major event

y attended. It was no secret who the Vado family was. They were

ed by some but hated by many. The Mexicans jumped into their

and sped off of the scene.

"Wi out." Kill called out to his brothers as they sprinted to

r car. Kill's mind raced and went a million miles per hour.

rything had escalated too quickly. Shit wasn't over, not by far.

streets were covered in blood, and blood meant death. They

Making sure that he saw his gang on standby, he s

brothers with two head nods letting them know shit was a

start popping off.

BANG!

As soon as the first shot rang out Sonny sobered

He pulled his gun out and started to return fire to any Me

saw. The Mexican's bullets shot like wildflower, hitting

sight. They were reckless. Akiel stared around making s

an eye on his brothers. They were all ducked down and

were taking over. It was a clear war between the Vado b

Mexican's. Every time they drop a Mexican it seemed l

one popped out of another clown car.

Although their shooters were returning fire, sor

were taking some heat. They were outnumbered. Bodie

dropping left and right, and Kill was well aware they d

long before the police got there. He let out a sharp whi

through the air, using his last resort it was time to cut a

way bullets flew around he knew it was time to shut it

were just getting started. A war was in motion and there was no

telling when it would end

Chapter 2

"Damn baby, this food smelling like it's good for my soul."
Badrick complimented as he took a seat at the head of the dining
table at his family restaurant Footprints. His wife Chermaine was the
head cook in his kitchen. Her hands spoke for themselves; Cher was
top of her class in culinary school. Food was the way to her heart
and it was the way to Rich's too. After he'd gotten a taste of her
cooking, he had to keep her. Cher was all woman, and Rich knew
that she was the one to wife up. If he didn't somebody else would
and he didn't want to add more bodies to his count for something he
could avoid. Cher was his, the 3 carat diamond ring said it all. He
loved everything about his woman. From the way she cooked, to the
way she fucked, and even the way her long hair fell down to the
middle of her back. Cher was a trophy in Rich's eyes, the one that
sat above all.

"Unh uh, this food is good for your belly, I feed your soul,"
She answered as she placed a bowl of fried dumplings onto the table.

"Ew ma," Their eleven-year-old daughter Chasity chimed in as she scrunched up her face. Rich and Cher laughed at her expense.

"Where are my uncles?" Legend, their five year old son asked as he shook his head full of shoulder length dreads. He was his daddy's son. Spitting image of Badrick but his heart was like Cher's.

"They went to a Summer Jam, without me," Chas joined in while rolling her eyes.

Rich couldn't help but laugh. "Gal wah you know bout Summa Jam?" His baby girl Chasity was growing up before his very eyes. She was eleven going on twenty one and Rich wanted to keep her as his baby forever. She was his first born, the apple of his eye.

"Mi know dat mi miss di best concert of di summer. Kamari been sending mi videos all day." Chasity answered with a frown on her face.

"Kamari's mother wears Kamari like she's a purse. She takes that little girl everywhere, and I mean everywhere. Summer Jam isn't for children. I'll take you probably when you turn sixteen. Now bow your head so we can say grace." Cher demanded as she grabbed

Legend and Chasity 's hand.

"God thank you for this food, and the hands you blessed me

with to put all this together. May it bless our souls and stick to all the

right places. Amen." Cher prayed while opening her eyes. Rich

stared at her with a smirk on his face. Everything about his wife

turned him on. The way her ass set in her jeans, the way her titties

damn near fell out her shirt and shit it's sad to say even the way she

prayed made him want to bend her over. If his kids weren't there he

probably would have had her spread eagle on the table. He would

have been eating, just not the food she cooked.

"Pass me the rice." She told him with playful grin on her

face. Rich knew his wife like the back of his hand. She was in a

good mood and it showed.

"Yuh having a good day?" He asked her and the smile on

Cher face answered his question. It kept the room brightened.

"It's been the first time in a long time that we've had dinner

with just us four. This feels good." Cher explained.

"Mi gone mek it right baby, mi gone mek more time for you. For the five of us." Rich reassured her, making her blush.

Cher was right, he couldn't remember the last time that his brothers hadn't been over for dinner. Being the oldest of the Vado brothers, Rich treated his brother's like his children. They were all under his wing. He was their protector. After the death of their parents, Rich had stepped up. Being the man of the house came like second nature. He'd grown up looking up to his father and how he protected and provided. Although his brothers were grown, Rich invited them over for dinner daily. He wanted them to eat together in all aspects of life. That was what family was supposed to do. Rich had started his own family tradition and following it had kept them all alive, got him a wife, and beautiful kids. Without his brother's there a small piece of him felt like a part of him was missing. But the look of content on Cher's face lessened the feeling. Sometimes he forgot about the family he created being so focused on the family he'd come from.

"Where's Enoch?" Rich asked, realizing that one of his cubs was missing.

"I fed him and put him to sleep." Cher responded while eating a mouthful of oxtails.

The sound of Rich's ringing phone pulled his attention. He dug into his pocket seeing an incoming call from Kill. "Waah happening Killa," He answered, putting the phone to his ears.

"Yo, were yuh at?" Kill asked, getting straight to the point. Rich heard Kill's accent coming out. Although his voice was calm, the change in accent was a trigger. It meant Kill caught a body or was about to catch one.

"Having dinna," Rich told him as he stood from the table walking towards the back office. Keeping business and the family he created out of it.

"Wi on our way. Shit hot."

Rich could hear Sonny in the background yelling, and he rubbed his temple. Sonny was hot headed. Rich could bet money that his little brother had set some shit off. From the way Kill sound, it was deadly. "Put mi on speaka," He ordered Kill.

"Talk," Kill told him. Sonny was getting on his fucking nerves. His temper had gotten them in some shit once again. Sonny was unpredictable. Hanging with him you didn't know if you'd make it alive another day.

"Carson chill di fuck out. Use yuh fucking head. Sit an think wah the fuck yuh do?" Rich barked into the phone.

"Waaaaah!!" Enoch wailed at the top of his lungs and Rich rushed over to him.

"Kill mek sure di tree of yuh walk in dis home. Kill off everybody if you have to." He ordered his brother before hanging up the phone.

"Badrick, come look at the news." Cher gave him a knowing look. Rich's temple throbbed as he followed his wife into the dining area and there it was.

"Breaking News: Gang shootout at Summer Jam, leaving fifteen people dead." Rich's eyes instantly went bloodshot red. He

turned to Cher passing Enoch to her. "Take di kids and go home. I'll be in late tonight."

Cher looked at him with worried eyes. Fifteen bodies. That wasn't something people would sweep under the rug. Fifteen bodies meant there would be smoke at their door. Whether it was the law or the streets. "Make sure you make it through those doors Badrick."

"These kids need you." She whispered to him. Rich placed his forehead onto hers looking into her glossy eyes. He could tell she was tired of this shit. Fearing if he would come home or end up in a ditch. She was living on edge. Cher didn't leave the house without two pistols on her. The life Rich lived made her and her children targets, that was the life of being married to a King. Accepting to be his Queen came with risk, and Cher had to be on her toes at all times. But being on her toes, working, and being a mom was all too much. She was used to being a regular girl that didn't have to stay strapped. Cher vowed to the risk of being married to a hood nigga in the name of love hoping that Rich would pull out from the game one day. But he never did, and she didn't know if he would ever.

"Yuh don't need mi?" He asked her. Cher stepped back, putting space between them. Before she could answer, the restaurant doors swung open and Kill, Nitro, and Sonny strolled in as if they hadn't just left over a dozen mothers childless.

"Chasity pack the food up, while I get your brothers ready to go." Cher said walking past her brother in laws without acknowledging them.

"What's good Cher?" Kill asked, recognizing the emotion in her eyes.

Cher ignored him as she led Legend into the kitchen to wash his hands.

"Tek a seat." Rich instructed his brothers as he nodded towards the booth. They waited for Cher and the kids to leave before Rich shot his eyes towards Sonny. "Speak."

"Bro, these Mexican niggas had me fucked up. This nigga bumped into me wasting his drink on my new fucking shoes." Sonny started and Rich's eyes turned black listening to his little brother, he wondered if Sonny could hear the words that were coming from his mouth.

"Yuh shoes, yuh shoes nigga? Yuh start shooting ova sum shoes! Yuh get funds Sonny! Go buy yuh ten pairs of shoes boy. Who di fuck dem anyways." Rich slammed his hands on the table, if his brothers was any other niggas they would have flinched. But they shook their heads. This shit was routine.

"How many times do I have to tell you I'm not a damn boy!" Sonny hated to be called a boy, there was no respect behind being seen as a child. "I don't know who they are, some Mexican niggas. I never seen them a day in my life."

"I never seen them either Rich, I know everybody out here and these niggas new here." Nitro finally spoke up because he was already tired of being there. He was supposed to be in some pussy right now and they were holding him up.

"Kill, find out who dem are, Mi need names, addresses."

"Already pon it."

"Nitro and Sonny, you can leave!" Rich dismissed his younger brothers while he and Kill sat back already knowing that a war was the last thing they needed. But bodies had been dropped "Yuh little brotha hotheaded, how wi gon fix it?"

"Rich, you know there's only one thing to calm that nigga down."

"Di nigga act like medicine poison but will smoke a bag of ganja like it curing him." Rich fussed as he rolled his blunt. Sonny had a problem, and instead of taking care of it. He neglected it and it always got them in some shit.

"That nigga is reckless Rich. The bodies we dropped today over some J's is ridiculous. He needs to take his meds or be put on a fucking leash."

Chapter 3

You wanna talks? You wanna run your mouth?

You want some gangstas front your muthaf house?

We'll set this off, yeah, set this off

We'll set this off, set this off

Sonny sped down the freeway with his sound system blaring catching everyone's attention. His icy blue 2020 mustang did 150 mph, as he swiftly switched lanes.The thrill of being so close to danger made Sonny feel free. It was the fate of having his life in his hands and playing with fire and winning that fight. He was feeling like that nigga and nobody could tell him nothing. Today was his favorite day of the week. Pick up day. He'd been to eight of the traps for pick up and he was finally at the last one. He couldn't wait to do his drop off so he could hit up the club and have a bad bitch in his lap. Sonny was young, fly and arrogant. The ladies made him that way. He hadn't seen a woman that he couldn't get yet. Even the older shorties wanted a piece of his young ass and Sonny loved every bit of it.

Once he pulled up to the trap, he pulled into the garage and put his gun in his waistband before he entered.

Loud.

Sonny knew the smell of the weed that they supplied. It had come straight from Jamaica; their family empire was in their blood. The weed was from their roots. The Vado family's weed farm had been supplying the states for over sixty years. The throne was passed down from their great great grandfather and down a line and it was now almost Rich's turn. Sonny dreamt of the day when it would be his turn to run their family's drug cartel. They had the game on lock with their potent weed which made it too easy. "Yo Block, I know my money better be right the way you smoking our shit like a nigga won't take it out your pay." Sonny grilled as he took the blunt from one of his lieutenants. He puffed on the blunt like Block had rolled it just for him.

"I just finished counting that shit up. It's all there in the bag." Block answered as he stood to his feet. Sonny looked at him like he was stupid.

"Nigga I know you better empty that muthafucking bag out and count it in my face,"

"C'mon Son, I've been doing this shit for eight years. Before you started pickups. You know my shit always counted up right." Block responded with a slightly offended look on his face. Sonny laughed as he blew the smoke out his mouth.

"Man, that's my fucking point. You been here too fucking long to be tryin to bullshit me. Now empty the fucking bag!" Carson yelled as he pulled his gun out aiming it at Block.

He watched as Block placed his hands in surrender and walked over to the bag picking it up. He emptied it out, onto the table. Sonny sat on the reclining chair already knowing that Block's life was on a time clock. Sonny's saw all kind of red flags and he knew a pussy nigga when he saw one. As he watched Block count up the money, the shakiness in his hand didn't go unnoticed. Like Block had said, he'd been with the Vado family for eight years and Sonny had never seen him fold. "Why do I have a feeling imma have to body you today?" Sonny asked calmly with a wide smile on his face. Killing made him happy, gave him a rush. It fed his anger. Killing Block would start his night off right.

He watched as the sweat poured out of Block's face.

"Nigga is your pores okay?" Sonny chuckled as he stood up.

"Y-yo Sonny. My daughter birthday came up and she wanted some extravagant shit, I needed to borrow a couple bands."

Sonny squinted his eyes as he neared Block putting his gun to his head. "What the fuck is a couple bands nigga? I been a kid before I don't remember ever needing a couple bands." Sonny growled in his ear.

"Okay, okay! Listen Sonny. This bad bitch I was fucking with wanted to go on a vacation and I told her I was going to cover it. All the money I make working for y'all going to my baby mama and my mama. I gotta make sure they straight, but I be trying to have a little fun. You never did nothing crazy for a piece of pussy man?" Sonny thought Block was crazy the way he was rambling off at the mouth. He was sure Block had lost his mind the minute the gun touched his temple. Sonny had waited hoping Block would make a good plea but he came up short.

"Nah nigga, I get pussy easily. I don't have to pay for shit. I could go tell yo mama to drop her panties for a nigga and I have her bent over dusting the cobwebs off her pussy."

Block was shaking in his boots and Sonny didn't feel an ounce of sympathy for him. Block has stolen their money and tried to get away with it. Sonny thought about how he had the bag sitting on the floor counted up and lied to his face about it. Sonny's nose flared. He would've preferred Block came to him like a man instead of sneaking like a bitch. He didn't get any respect from Sonny.

"Fif-"

Pow!

Sonny put a hole in Blocks head leaving him slumped over the table. He quickly walked to the front of the trap. "City come put all this bread back in the bag for me. And y'all clean this nigga up." Sonny ordered the other guys who bagged up the weed. "Y'all niggas know it's two things I don't play about. My weed and my money. I don't know why this nigga thought today was gone be a good day when he was playing with both."

Sonny watched as everyone did as he said, and it brought joy to his heart. Feeling like the king of something so important, like his family's empire made him feel good. He wanted to be the king of the jungle. He'd watched Rich rule the streets and drop more bodies than he could count. His no tolerance for bullshit came from watching his older brother and looking up to him.

Once City passed him the bag Sonny walked out leaving them to deal with the mess he made. Sonny turned his speakers up as he blasted A Boogie's *Jungle*. "Nigga this is what that jungle do.

You been plottin' nigga, wasn't you?" The song took Sonny to another world as he thought of all the possible outcomes if he hadn't been on his game. Block would've robbed them and possibly killed them in the long run. He had nip the shit in the bud quickly not giving another nigga the thought of trying them. He'd made an example of Block.

Sonny's gut took him out of his thoughts when he looked through his rear-view mirror and a blacked-out dodge followed him. *Pussy ass niggas trying to catch me slipping*. He thought to himself. He quickly made his way onto the freeway doing 190 mph dodging cars by a millisecond. The dodge follows him precisely. Anyone would've thought that the two cars were racing but, no. Somebody was on Sonny's ass and he was determined to lose them. He pressed a button that put the roof back in its place not wanting to be as accessible as he started.

He dialed Rich's number on Bluetooth knowing that his brother would have a plan, he always did. Sonny had too much money on him to get caught by the niggas after him or the police.

"Richie, some niggas is following me and I can't shake them." Sonny told him as soon as the phone started ringing.

"Weh yuh at?" Rich asked as he made his way to his car with no further questions. The thought of his brother in danger haunted him. Although Sonny was a fuck up Rich rode for his brothers. His parents left his brothers in his care and he'd be damned if somebody was trying to body his brother. Especially his baby brother.

"I'm coming off 285 heading into the city."

"Mi and Nitro gon meet yuh there. Turn yuh location on, and go inna secluded area," Rich instructed, and Sonny followed his brother's direction.

POW POW POW!! Bullets began to come crashing towards Sonny's car and he smirked when his bullet proof windows didn't crack. He prepared for shit like this. He was too young to die and a reckless nigga. Although he was flashy, Sonny's safety was first. Sonny knew what his temper was capable of and as long as he was in his car he was safe.

Once the bullets stopped, he slowed his car down and slowly leaned out the window letting the dodge pass him as he rolled down a window letting a shot out. *Dumb ass nigga wasted all his bullets.* Now Sonny saw why Rich said every nigga wasn't made for the game.

BANG BANG

Sonny put two into the drivers head and watched as the car went out of control into an intersection. Before Sonny could put his car to a complete stop.

BOOM!

Rich's 2019 Jeep Grand Cherokee collided into the side of the dodge causing it to flip over.

"Yo!!!!" Sonny hollered amazed at the scene at hand. His fist under his mouth like a mic and his mouth in an *o* shape revealed his excitement. Sonny felt like he was watching a 3D movie starring him and his brothers.

Nitro hopped out his car and laughed at Rich. "Why it look like you been waiting all your life to do some shit like that?"

"Man, yuh have no clue what mi have dun in dis life." Rich answered with a grin on his face as he walked over to the dodge and pulled the passenger out. The driver was DOA and the backseat passenger groaned because of the impact while trying to reach for his gun.

"Dis boy got heart, fighting to him dying second go a hell boy." Rich sneered as he put two in his head.

"Well, well, well, look what we have here" Rich smirked as he held the last bloodied Mexican teen. He didn't know who he was. But Rich was determined to find out, one way or another.

***

Kill pulled up to Cher and Rich's house with his blunt in his mouth ready to plan Rich's birthday party. Two things his brother hated were surprises and birthdays. It was a reminder that he was in fact getting older and a little closer to the inevitable. So when Cher called Kill over to help plan Rich a night to remember he couldn't pass up the opportunity.

He stepped out of his car donning a pair of crisp white Air Force ones and a pair of Amiri shorts with a white T and a rag over his shoulder. His locs fell over his shoulders and a bucket hat covered his head. The Atlanta sun was burning him up. He made his way to the backyard where he could hear the kids and Cher playing in their in-ground pool.

Kill stopped at the gate and began to admire the family that his brother created. Kill wanted that one day, but he feared commitment. After dealing with one scornful woman, she'd made an imprint on his life. Kill had vowed to never settle down. But how else would he get the picture-perfect family that would play in a pool while he was working hard.

"Uncle Kill, come get in the pool with us." Chasity called her uncle while dipping her head underwater and swimming to the other end of the pool. Her swimming classes had surely paid off as she turned into a human mermaid in her element.

"Not today, I have some work I have to do. I'll come back tomorrow and I'm all yours." He persuaded her. Kill didn't want to tell his niece no, but it was time to get down to business. He had a busy day and the time slot he and Cher had set up to plan was ticking.

"Yo sis, you wanna get out the pool and come sit down so we can go over this party?" Cher stepped out of the pool looking like she was a Gucci model the way the two piece hugged her frame. Her milk chocolate skin was glistening from the water and the sun shining down on her was doing her justice. The smile and simple combo was one that any man had to escape before getting consumed in it because Cher was just that charming.

Kill tilted his head back realizing that his thought had almost gotten the best of him. Cher was off limits in every aspect of family, and bro code.

Cher walked over to the outdoor bar with Enoch on her hip as she made a drink for her and Kill. She motioned for Kill to come over to where she was sitting.

Once he sat on the stool she sat Enoch on the counter. "Okay, let's start." Cher pulled her iPad from behind the bar and pulled up the information she needed on it.

Kill waited to hear her ideas as he bounced his nephew in his lap. "So, I would have the party here, but I know how Rich is about having too many people at our house. How do you feel about shutting down Footprints and having it there?" As Cher spoke Kill fell victim to getting lost in between her lips and her voice. Shit was soothing and Kill hadn't realized how easily she'd hypnotized him. "Kill...Kill?" Snapping her fingers, she finally got his attention.

Kill couldn't believe that for a second time in one day he was getting lost in Cher. He didn't know what it was. This was the first and it scared him. *I need to get some more sleep.* He thought of a solution to his problem before responding. "Uh, yeah, we can do it at Footprints. Do you want to cater it, or do you want to get it catered?"

"Now boy, you know damn well I'm not letting no one cater this event when I can cook my damn self." Laughing Kill raised his hands up to let Cher know he didn't want any smoke.

"Okay, don't kill me killer." Cher laughed at him and shook her head, if she had to pick her favorite brother-in-law, he was it no doubt. Kill was the most mature. He and Rich were the closest, and if she vented to anyone about Rich it was Kill. All the time he spent at their house made it easy to be comfortable around one another.

He looked down at his phone, and noticed that Nitro was calling him. He ignored it and sat his phone on the bar top then turned back to Cher to finish going over their plans when his phone rang again. This time it was Rich calling so something wasn't right. He sat Enoch onto the counter while putting his phone to his ear.

"Talk to me bro."

"Meet me at di restaurant now, wi ave business to handle! Red." Kill jumped up immediately. He knew red meant blood. It was code for someone trying to take one of them out.

"Cher, imma have to link up with you another day this week. Book everything and just send me the bill." Kill instructed as he rushed out.

He jumped into his car and made what would've been a thirty-minute ride, a fifteen-minute. The entire way there he smoked his blunt trying to figure out what happened without any of the details. The fact that somebody tried to take out one of his brothers enraged him. He wondered if it were the Mexicans from Summer Jam or some new niggas. Hell, with Sonny ass for a brother anything was possible.

Once he pulled up to the restaurant, Kill went around back and put in his code so he could be let in. He made his way into the basement of the restaurant and heard somebody groaning out in pain.

"Who the fuck are you and who sent you after me?" Sonny hit the Mexican guy over the head with an empty Hennessy bottle that sat on the table.

"Vete a la Mierda, no digo nada." (Fuck you I'm not saying shit)The man sitting in the chair spit out blood getting it on Sonny's shoes, making him even madder than he was.

Sonny grabbed a pair of brass knuckles, and slid his fingers through them as he began to beat the man to a pulp. Kill stood back in shock as he noticed the man still wasn't talking. Although Sonny was putting the beat down on him, the man was a soldier. Kill was into the sport of working smarter not harder. He walked over to the closet and pulled out a rusted bat with nails sticking out. Walking over to where the man was, Kill brought the bat down onto his leg.

"Ahhh fuck. Puta just kill me." You could see the pain in his eyes and could tell that he just wanted to get it over with. But Kill didn't have any intention of obliging.

"Nah, the fun just getting started." Smiling Kill went into his pocket and pulled out his Spec Arc Pocket knife that would get the job done. "Untie this bitch ass nigga."

Nitro walked over to the man and stood behind him untying his arm while making sure he didn't make any sudden moves.

"We're about to play a little game. Rich is going to ask you a question and if I don't like your answer then you lose a finger. If you don't speak at all you lose the whole hand. You ready?" The man still didn't speak and Kill shrugged swiftly slicing one of his fingers off.

"Ahhhhh," the man's screams filled the basement and Kill silently thanked God it was soundproof. Rich pulled up a chair and sat right in front of the mexican, leaving room for Kill to do what he had to do.

"Who sent yuh?" Looking Rich in the eyes he didn't say a word. Instead his mug deadlier when he was in no shape or form to be sending silent threats.

"I ave to give it to him brudda, Him ave heart." Kill complimented the guy while shaking his head. He used the knife slicing through his wrist joint and watched as his hand fell onto the floor.

"Ahhhh, just kill me, please just kill me." He was losing so much blood that he was slipping in and out of consciousness. "Yo

Sonny, go grab a bucket of water so we can wake this nigga up."
Nitro spoke up for the first time, he had shit to do today and it didn't
include torturing this punk ass nigga.

"Wake yo ass up, I don't have all day." Nitro poured the
water on his head so he could wake up. Barely opening his eyes, he
looked around at the men before him.

"Yuh muss really nuh like yo life. Dem niggas yuh saving
worth yuh life?" Rich chuckled as the stubborn soldier. He nodded
towards Kill so he could get ready to cut some more fingers off.

The man groaned out in pain and as he turned his neck Kill
saw a tattoo that read *DeLeon*.

"Rich, Look a dis." Rich stepped back and shook his head as
he looked at the man's neck.

"Please tell mi yuh didn't start nuttin wid di DeLeon Cartel."
Pacing the floor, Rich had his brothers looking at him sideways. All
of them were confused as to why Rich's attitude shifted so quickly.

"Who the fuck is the DeLeon Cartel and why the fuck do you care? These niggas tried to have me killed and you worried about them." Sonny scoffed in disgust as he looked at the man and punched him again.

"DeLeon for life Puta." The guy smirked through bloody lips. The cockiness in his tone enraged Sonny a little more. It was too identical to his cocky, and Rich had shown fear. But Sonny wasn't backing down. He was tired of the man's mouth. Sonny grabbed Kill's bat and connected it with the man's face, breaking his neck on impact.

Crack!

The sound was music to Sonny's ears as he beat him until he was unrecognizable. Kill walked towards the closet and pulled out his Machete. He grabbed the man by his battered head and swung the machete cutting his neck off.

"Clean tis shit up." Rich walked out the restaurant wondering how he was about to clean up the real mess his brothers made.

Chapter 4

Nitro and Sonny stepped into their family's underground club. It was hot, and the only safe place to be. It was for VIP personnel only. You had to be in a different tax bracket to be in there. It was a room full of hustlers just jamming, smoking weed, cigars, drinks, hookahs you name it. There were a few lady hustlers, who dwindled in their own booths and they all looked like they earned the right to be there if they weren't a boss; they were the wife of one.

"I got eyes on shorty to the right in the booth, so stay your young ass at this bar for a nigga okay?" Nitro whispered in his brother's ear as they took a seat on the barstool.

"Damn nigga, I had eyes on shorty."

Nitro looked at Sonny with a sarcastic look knowing that Sonny was looking to bust a nut and keep it pushing. He would stick his dick in just about anything with a pussy and two legs. He was young, rich, and loved fucking bitches. He would try to fuck every woman in the underground if he could no matter what beef it brought. Nitro had spotted one woman while Sonny spotted them all. It was why Nitro needed his brother to act as normal as he could and try to not let his ego fuck their night up.

"Bro, just chill, it's mad bad bitches in here. One for me ten for you." Nitro joked as he waved down the bottle girl. "Troi, do me a favor and bring Sonny a bottle of Don Julio, it makes him nice." Nitro winked at her as he walked over to the light domican bred woman that sat in a booth all alone slowly pulling on her hookah.

"What's poppin hookah mami?" Nitro greeted as he slid beside her. The corners of her lips turned into a small smile.

"What's poppin lil daddy," She replied as she blew the smoke into his face. Nitro could see the fire dancing in her eyes and it intrigued him. She was openly flirting unlike most women. Like she knew she was the shit and was waiting to see which nigga was gone step to her. He licked his lips leaning over into her ear.

"Aint nothing lil about a nigga," He told her honestly, her light cheek's blushed. She too could feel the danger between the engagement of the two of them. Everything about Nitro looked bad. He was a fine ass light skin nigga with thick back length bleached locs, a baguette, grills, and swag. His tattoos that covered his arms and neck made her assume he loved pain to make pleasure. Their energies gravitated to one another. She inhaled the hookah as she placed her hand on his thigh. She was deciding to make the first move. *Always have one up on these niggas* she thought. She wasn't into wasting her time and as much as she wanted to fuck with Nitro because of the brief energy exchanged, she had to make sure he wasn't bluffing.

When her pretty fingers felt the bulge in his pants, she wasted no time. "What's your name?" She asked wanting to skip the introductory part, and straight to the fucking. But she had to be a lady first. Everything in her was telling her to go fuck him in the stall, even though that wasn't how her mama raised her. She wanted him to take her to the bathroom rip off her panties and fuck her until she dried up, which would be a while. They would probably be fucking until the bar closed.

"Nitro," All the respect she had for herself went out the window, she wanted to fuck, and she wanted to fuck now.

"Genie," She told him before standing up. *Fuck being a lady.* She thought to herself as she led the way to the bathroom. Something told her that if she put it down on his fine ass good enough, she'd hear from him again. Genie didn't know what made her want to do Nitro so bad. Maybe it was because she hadn't gotten any good dick in a long time and Nitro just looked like he had dick for sale walking around with big dick energy. She could tell his money was long from all the jewels he wore. But she was confident that her money was longer. So, she wasn't looking for anything more than a good time.

Nitro stood up like a dog with his tongue out, tail wagging and ready to bite a piece of steak. Nitro was fluent in sex. Genie walked away so he could follow and send her to the moon with his dick. He watched as she headed towards the bathroom and a cocky grin appeared on his face as he followed her into the bathroom.

Once he walked in Genie held her thongs in her hand giving a Nitro a visual of her backside. Nitro had fucked badder bitches, bitches with bigger ass and titties, but never a bitch with as much confidence as Genie. Genesis DeLeon had the confidence of a hundred bad bitches and her body was natural. Her face was pretty, and her money was long.

Nitro walked over to her using his hand to round her ass before placing his finger in between the slit of her pussy. Genie was wet and ready without a spit start pussy. Every part of Nitro wanted to fill her up with dick, but the aroma of her wetness invaded his nose. He was like a dog with a bone. He wanted to taste it and make sure it was just right for him before he dug himself a hole. Nitro spun Genie around and sat her onto the porcelain sink. He kneeled getting eye level with her budding rose. Genie looked edible and Nitro couldn't hold himself back as he parted her lips. Genie's back arched as his tongue feasted on her like he'd gotten an A plus in head. Like he'd studied and mastered how to eat pussy. "Ahhhh,"

Genie moaned as she fisted his locs. She grinded her pussy into his face while slyly smirking. Looking into her eyes while sucking on her clit made Genie cum all over his tongue and while her eyes rolled to the back of her head.

Yes eat this fucking fat cat boy. She thought to herself. Nitro stood up and his jeans were already at his ankles and a condom coated his dick. He'd prepared himself while satisfying Genie and it only turned her on more. Nitro knew how to not make shit be awkward. He was straight to the point like she was.

Nitro's body temperature rose as he entered Genie's walls. He closed his eyes as her warm tightness took over his mind for a split second. *This bitch got the devil's pussy.* Nitro thought as he slowly eased in and out of her. He made sure to make every thrust felt, as Genie moaned in his ear. Her pleasure hypnotized him. Her tongue grazed his lips and as much as Nitro wanted to turn away, he couldn't. Genie and her demon pussy had put a hex on him. Making him go against everything he truly stood for. He wasn't a bathroom fucking nigga but here she had him moving against himself already. Genie's eyes rolled to the top of her head as she bounced on his dick.

Nitro grabbed her neck firmly. As their tongues danced around and they exchanged their lust, the both of them felt the orgasm coming. Nitro pumped harder as Genie bounced catching his speed. She was so close to the moon, already near the stars *again*. When Nitro pulled out and blew in her pussy placing his fingers inside of her, he played with her clit and Genie exploded. "Oh my fucking god." Genie whispered as she came down from her high.

Nitro stood back and licked her wetness off his lips. "Like a nigga said, aint shit little about me." He pulled the condom off his dick while Genie cleaned herself up.

"Two for two?" She asked with a raised brow. She wanted to see how far Nitro could go. This was her first-time having bathroom sex and it was the best sex she'd received in her life. All she could wonder was if that's what he could do in a bathroom. He was the king of the bedroom.

Nitro chuckled as he shook his head slightly amused by Genie's sex drive. "You don't even know what you about to get yourself into ma." He said as he walked up on her.

"I wanna find out. You haven't even received this fire head from me. Let's make it a challenge, lets see who can make the other cum first." She told him leading the way.

Nitro walked over to Sonny who sat at the bar having casual conversation with the bartender Troi. The sight of Sonny so calm excited him, he wouldn't have to babysit if his brother could hold it down. Nitro wondered if it was Troi or if the war had shaken his brother up.

"I'm about to break out with shorty. She feenin for the dick already. You gucci, or you tryna break out."

"Nigga I'm grown. Go on and get ya dick wet. I'm chilling." Sonny told him with his eyes low. Nitro was good at reading his brother, and he could tell Sonny was in a chill mood.

"He can stay with me until my shift is over. I'll make sure he gets home." Troi chimed in, taking charge like she wanted his company.

A low grin tugged the corners of Sonny's lips as he turned his attention back to Troi. He licked his lips and tilted his head to the side trying to figure out her angle. She'd held his attention since the minute he sat at the bar and he wasn't mad at it. Troi's approach was much more different than other women. She'd shot down his every attempt to get at her, but she was willing to let him take her home. He wondered if it was the four-year age gap that made him want her more. He didn't know what he wanted with her, but he'd always been up for a chase and Troi's had piqued his interest. Troi seemed like she had everything that he wanted, from her looks to the way her ass jiggled when she was walking.

Nitro chuckled as he looked at his brother stunned. It amused him, he finally realized that the war hadn't gotten him to chill. It was Troi. He had his sights on the brown beauty. "Aight bro, hit me up when you get in." Nitro told him as he followed Genie out of the underground.

Sonny leaned back in his chair letting one leg down from the stool as he folded his arms across his chest and nodded over at Troi with his eyes in a squint. "You wanna keep playing with me?"

"Boy I am too old to be playing games with you." Troi challenged him and she placed both of her elbows onto the counter as a wide smile graced her face. She was beautiful, she knew it and Sonny did as well. He hadn't gotten up not because of Nitro but because he really wanted Troi. Her beauty put her in a caliber above the rest. Beauty like hers he'd only seen in pictures. Specific pictures of his late mother. Troi had the same brown locs, and fair skin. It had held his attention, and her vibe felt familiar.

"I usually don't like that boy word. But imma let you slide. You could call me boy, baby, daddy whichever you prefer." Sonny leaned into her getting up in her face close. Their eyes locked in on one another. Sonny was in a trance. Swirling in the pool of honey in her eyes.

"Yo Troi, the homie tryna holla at you." A voice cut through the air breaking up their connection. Sonny's nose flared as he stood in his seat over the man grilling him. He recognized him.

"Solo, you don't see me talking to shorty?" Sonny yoked him up bringing up four more inches till they were at eye level.

"M-my fault Sonny. I ain't mean no disrespect bro. I-I ain't know." Solo stuttered as he put his hand up in defense. He truly hadn't read the room if he had he would've noticed that Sonny was chilling. But cutting in on his moment was like Solo poked a bear.

"Which one of your friends?" Troi's voice caused Sonny's neck to snap towards her. He let go of Solo abruptly causing him to stumble backwards.

"Why you wanna know which one?"

"Cause if I'm checking for any nigga it's not the one that turn into the fucking hulk cause someone approached me."

"With all due respect, I don't give a fuck about none of that shit ma. Talk to them niggas out there. In here, you only talking to me. And if a nigga bold enough to step to you in front of me again, Imma"

"What? You gon do what? Boy you are not my man."

"Yet," Sonny smirked cutting her off. Troi's voice was caught in her chest and he leaned into her one more. "This little boy will fuck you into a wheelchair or fuck yo life up. Whichever you prefer."

Troi's pearl throbbed, she could feel her panties getting wet. Sonny was aggressive, straight to the point, young and cocky.

"And that's why yo young asss ain't getting a peace of this pussy." She told him matter factly as she walked away from him. She had no choice. The closer she was to him the more she was wrapped up in his charm and a little distance was needed. Because Sonny was a bad boy. He'd warned her ahead of time and showed her firsthand. And Troi would take heed because with Sonny there was no telling when he'd turn green. He was a ticking time bomb that she didn't want to be near when it exploded.

***

One thing Rich hated doing was getting on planes and jets. Heights wasn't his thing. Although he owned a private jet he hated it with a passion. Going to Jamaica wasn't in his plans. The trip had come unexpected, but Rich had an idea about why he was being called down by his uncle. He was next in line to run their family operation from Jamaica. The family weed farm was a throne and needed to be passed down by the head of the hierarchy. When his uncle Llanzo called he had to be on the first thing smoking.

"Mr. Rich, here are you and your guest bags. Is there anything else I can do for you this evening?"

"No sir, you enjoy your stay in Jamaica. Everything is on me." Rich nodded his head at his pilot as they went their separate ways.

"I'm really in your hometown bae, thank you for bringing me." Missy linked her arm into his as they made their way to the car that was waiting on them. Rich knew he was fucked up bringing his mistress with him instead of his wife and kids. But Cher was holding the restaurant down and the kids had school. He'd promised Missy a vacation and there was no better place to vaca than Jamaica.

"I told yuh, I had yuh. Believe in mi." Leaning down he kissed her on her lips. Rich loved Missy because she was secure in her position as the side bitch. It made him want and crave her more.

He and Cher rarely got into it and whenever he was having a bad day Missy was there to suck his soul from his dick and restore it into his body. Missy held a special place in his heart and although he never admitted it, the things he did for her spoke volumes. He'd brought her out to his hometown where everyone knew he was married.

"We're free to be together here, we don't have to worry about anything. It's me and you. Since you said we're staying on a private beach, I can't wait until I can fuck you in the sand." Missy said in a seductive tone. Rich hardened at the thought of her riding him during the sunset on a beach, he was ready for business to be over so he could be with her the way he wanted to.

"Let mi handle business then mi all yours." Opening the car door that was waiting for him, he let Missy get in first so he could get a nice view of her ass as she bent down to get in. Their car ride to the beach house was silenced. Everyone sat in their own worlds.

Missy was thinking about all the nasty things she was going to do to Rich and all of the stuff he was going to buy her. Rich, was thinking about what Llanzo wanted with him, and the driver thinking what the fuck was going on and where Cher was. Rich didn't know that his uncle driver had clear instructions to bring him and his *wife* straight to his home, this clearly isn't the woman that was in the picture that he showed him.

"Wear wi headed di beach house di other way mon." Rich looked behind him confused.

"Mih wa given instructions to bring yuh tuh yuh uncle home." Shaking his head Rich, leaned back into his seat preparing himself for the bullshit that his uncle was about to take him through.

"Oh my gosh, Rich this is so nice. Why didn't we just stay here." Missy was amazed looking out the window.

"Listen whatever happens here, don't let it bother you. You only speak when spoken to, do mih make myself clear." Missy swallowed the lump in her throat and nodded her head. Stepping out of the car behind Rich, she walked behind him as they made their way to the front door.

"Mih Nefew, how are yuh." Llanzo swung open the front door greeting his oldest nephew. As he pulled Rich in for a hug when he looked over his shoulder his face became shock when he saw a woman who wasn't Cher.

"Uncle Llanzo, how yuh!"

Llanzo ignored his nephew; he looked straight at Missy with a scowl on his face. "No Whore in mih house, yuh can leave." he barked angrily. He couldn't believe that Rich was walking around with another woman on his arm when he had a loyal wife like Cher. If Missy was lighter, she would have been red in the face, but her dark skin made it hard for them to see how embarrassed she was.

"I'll wait in the car, handle yo business." Walking back to the car she had tears coming to her eyes. Never in her life had she ever been embarrassed like that; this was the one time in her life that she was ashamed to be a mistress. Even though she didn't like the way she was feeling, she knew she would never leave Rich alone. Missy wiped her eyes feeling like an outcast. She climbed into the car and pulled out her phone to occupy her time until Rich was done.

Inside the house Rich took a seat in front of his uncle's desk. "Yuh not right Unc, how could yuh do dat to her."

"Neva question me bwoy. Wat's been going on in da states."

"Sonny started some petty shit with the DeLeon's. Dey came afta him. Wi killed one of them. Mih don't know exactly who, but he was a DeLeon. His name was Jose." That one sentence alone made His uncle sit his drink down.

"Di DeLeon's. Have yuh lost Yuh mind. I though yuh had yuh brothers unda control. Yuh di oldest Rich, how could yuh let dis happen."

"Mih? Mih? Mih brothers are grown men. Dey do as dey please, Mih can't stop them." By now Rich was furious, He knew he didn't come all the way to Jamaica to get blamed for his brother's doings.

"Yuh are in charge in di states Rich, dem is yuh problem. Yuh need to fix it, or mih is coming to dih states and mih know yuh don't want that." He waited for Rich to respond and when he didn't, he continued, "Who is she and where is Chermaine?"

"She's just a friend."

"Mih and my brudda taught you to neva lie, look ah man right in his eyes when yuh speak tuh him. Look at mih and tell mih she's just a friend." Blowing out a breath Rich looked at his uncle.

"She's my side piece. I ave fun wit her and send her on her way. Mih buy her nice tings and then go home to mih wife. Yuh didn't call mih down here tuh be in mih business." Rich fussed tired of his uncle talking down on him. Rich was over being there already.

"Mi was stepping down, but mi see mi can't do dat anymore. Mi cant trust yuh to let down mi and mi brother legacy. Until yuh can prove tuh mi that yuh can handle mi business. Mi staying in the game. Get yuh brother together, get rid of di whore and make tis shit right. Go back home, yuh don't deserve tuh have fun. Yuh ave a week before mi is in the states Rich." Llanzo ordered without giving Rich a chance to speak any more. He walked away dismissing him.

As Rich walked out of the mansion, he began thinking of ways to fix it and the first thing he had to do was get Sonny to act right. All this shit could have been avoided but his dumb ass hotheaded brother didn't know when enough was enough.

Chapter 5

Nitro pulled up to Genie's house after leaving a family meeting. He was done with his work for the day, so he and Genie had made plans. Since the underground sex, sex between them made sparks fly. Their sexual energy kept them coming back to one another. When he pulled up to her house, he was surprised that she was living the way she was, her house was lavish from the outside. Close enough to a castle. Nitro stepped out of his car and made sure his gun was on his hip. He could never be too safe with the shit he and his brothers were going through.

Opening the door Genie admired Nitro. Dressed in some simple true religion shorts, a true religion white shirt and a pair of a white forces, he looked good enough to eat. *This man gets finer and finer.*

"Damn ma, you gone let me in or you gone keep looking at me like you about to fuck me right here." Snapping out of her trance she smacked her lips and moved to the side so he could come in.

"Make yourself comfortable," She told him taking a seat beside him. Nitro was already a step ahead of her with his feet propped up on her table and laid back on her couch.

"I already did ma, what you been up to today."

"I been with my family all day, my cousin has been missing. And my family comes from a world where no news is bad news. We hoping to hear something but deep down we all know that he's gone." Wiping a tear from her eye she got up and went to get her a bottle of water. "You want something to drink? I have water, juice, beer, wine, and Hennessy."

"For one, I'm a grown ass man, I don't drink wine, two a water is good." Rolling her eyes she walked back over to him and he pulled her on his lap. "On the real though, I'm sorry about your cousin, if something happens to one of mine, I know I'd be going crazy, so you handling this good." Leaning into him, Genie wrapped her arms around his neck and laid her head on his shoulders. Tensing up Nitro just let her lay there, this was a little too intimate for him, but she was hurting and even though he was an asshole, he didn't want to be one at the moment. Women were sensitive beings and Genie was vulnerable. Her usual attitude was out the window and it was clear her cousin's disappearance was weighing heavily on her.

"You know what, get dressed let's go out and have some fun. You know how to skate?" Nitro stood up with Genie legs wrapped around his waist.

"No, do you?"

"Do I know how to skate, baby I'm a king when it comes to skating. Go get sexy, so we can go and have some fun." Jumping down Genie rushed to her room to get herself together.

As she entered her closet, she was stuck trying to find something to wear. She knew she couldn't wear a dress and heels, and it was too damn hot to wear some pants. Settling on some high waist true religion shorts, she paired it with a plain white crop top and put on a pair of sandals. Going into her drawer she pulled out some socks to throw in her purse since they were going skating. Looking in the mirror, she put her long hair into a high bun and put on a nude color lips gloss and went back into the living room.

"I told you to get dressed not come out here matching my fly. You look good ass fuck though ma." Genie grabbed her purse and put her socks in it standing by the door.

"You coming or you gone keep looking at my ass." She didn't even turn around to face him and she already knew where his eyes were glued too. Walking up behind her, he wrapped his hands around her waist and whispered in her ear.

"Keep popping off at the mouth and I'm gone put something big in it." Turning to face him she smiled at him. The sexual energy between them was on fire, but they were just having fun.

"Keep licking yo lips like that and I'm gone give you something to lick." Nitro licked his lips again, taunting her as he gave her his famous smirk. "Bring yo ass on boy."

"After you." Nitro walked behind Genie and waited for her to lock her house up before escorting her to his car.

Nitro and Genie talked like old friends as he drove on the highway to their destination. They laughed and bonded about family, creating a genuine friendship between the two of them. They both left out important parts of their life but said just enough to seem normal. When they finally made it to the arena, Genie found herself thinking about what life would be like if she was his girl.

"You ready to learn how to skate." Nitro looked down on Genie as he stood in front of her with his skates on.

"Um, yeah. I guess."

"Well, if you guess than put the skates on woman. The first part to learning how to skate is putting on the skates." He spun in his skates like he was in Roll Bounce as he turned back to face her.

"I told you I was the king at skating ma, put yo skates on."

"Help me." She pouted when her nails wouldn't cooperate with putting the skates on. "I agreed to skating, not breaking a nail."

Nitro sat beside Genie, and she put her legs in his lap as he helped her with her skates. Once she stood up, she fell right back on her ass and Nitro tried his hardest not to laugh at her. "See, this why I never go skating." Pulling herself up she held onto Nitro for dear life.

"Come on, lets head to the floor. I got you." Holding her by her waist he led her to the floor and then took her hand. "You gotta relax ma."

"How am I supposed to relax when I can feel myself about to bust my ass. Nitro please don't let me fall again." Smirking Nitro let go of her and took off skating around the floor. Genie was agitated as she struggled to skate towards the exit of the skating floor. She sat down and watched Nitro skate. For him to be a hood nigga, skating looked like it brought him some type of peace and she enjoyed watching him out there on the floor.

Genie slipped off her skates and put on her sandals, she went to the concession stand to get him something to drink. "Can I get, ummmmm, two cherry freezies please and two slices of pizza." She paid and waited to get their stuff, then headed back to their table and waved Nitro down.

"You don't pay for nothing when you're with me. I appreciate it though." Blushing Genie sipped on her freezie and the things that crossed Nitro's mind had him ready to take her fine ass to the bathroom and fuck her in the stall *again*. "You betta stop sucking on the straw like that before we don't make it to laser tag."

"Forget laser tag, let's go and play basketball in the gaming room."

"I'm not trying to embarrass you out here now. Let's go though." Nitro and Genie ate and got rid of their trash then made their way to the arcade. This wasn't the type of date that Genie was used to but this was the best date that she's ever been on. She couldn't wait to school Nitro in basketball. A lot of men saw the heels, pretty face, long nails, and thought she couldn't hoop. After busting Nitro ass in basketball, Genie floated for all the shit he talked as he led her to play laser tag.

"It's going to be okay. I've been playing basketball since I was ten. I'm kind of a natural." She bumped him and he smiled at her. He didn't know what it was about her, but he fucked with her. She was cool as hell and her pussy was good.

"You can go chill, while I go get the laser tag tickets."

As Nitro walked over to the Laser tag stand, he saw a familiar face. Nitro doubled back as his main bitch Imani stepped into the bathroom behind the laser tag stand and his heart raced. Seeing the girl who had most of his attention, had his heart in his pocket. Imani was crazy as hell and seeing him with another female there was sure to set her off. Nitro wasn't about taking women's risk in public. Imani wouldn't hesitate to pop Genie in the mouth and Nitro wasn't sure exactly what Genie would do. And instead of finding out Nitro headed back towards his date.

"Yo, the laser tag line long as hell. You ready to go?" Nodding her head, they returned their skates and headed out the door. "Let's go get some takeout so we can go back to your house and chill.

"That's fine with me, what's good here?" Nitro Opened the door for her to get in the car then jogged around to the other side to get in.

"Let's go to This Is It BBQ and Seafood." As much as he wanted to take her to his brother's restaurant, he changed his mind. He wasn't ready to have Genie on his arm around his family. Dinner was for wifey and Genie wasn't that.

"Seafood is always good. Let's go." Nitro sped off doing 100 mph on the freeway. He and Genie vibed to music as the speed from the car gave them both a slight rush.

Nitro pulled off the highway and took the streets to the takeout spot. He parked in the fire lane and stepped out. "Denetro this is what we doing?" Imani's voice cut through the air. Nitro's stomach sank as he realized she spotted him before he spotted her. Before he could answer Genie stepped out of the car with a smirk on her face.

"And who is this?" Imani's voice was fed up as she crossed her arms on her chest waiting on him to open his mouth. But Nitro stood silent for the first time in his life he aint have shit to say. "Nitro, I know you about to introduce me to your new friend."

"Imani, don't start no shit. Get back in yo car and leave." Nitro tried de-escalating the problem before it even started.

"Hi, I'm Imani Nitro's girlfriend." Imani walked over to Genie and held out her hand so she could shake it.

"Hi. I'm Genie, Nitros future." Genie folded her arms and looked at Imani's hand like she had shit on it. "I'm hungry baby, you ready to go eat." Genie walked over to Nitro and looped her arm in his. Nitro was stuck because he knew Imani was with the shit. *5..4..* He counted down on the seconds he'd have until Imani lost her shit. She tied her hair in a bun, and walked towards Genie and her cousin Zina jumped out the car and pulled her back towards it.

"He's not worth it Mani, Let's go. Now! I'm not going to jail for you." Imani was out here about to show her ass. Nitro knew he was wrong for not going after Imani, but Imani had to understand that she wasn't his girl. The introduction she'd given had left a bad taste in his mouth wanting to create space between them. He felt like he could do as he pleased although if the roles were reversed he would've been on her neck.

"Bitch imma see you again! And when I do imma fuck you up!" Imani threatened as she tried her hardest to get away from Zina, but she couldn't. Genie and Nitro started walking towards the seafood place and Genie turned her head and smiled at Imani blowing her a kiss.

"Bring yo petty ass on." Nitro pulled Genie in the building. "You didn't look scared at all. Let me find out you a baby thug."

"I don't fear no bitch who bleeds just like I do. I don't appreciate you putting me in that predicament though. You lucky the dick go crazy, or I would've sent you on yo way after you fed me." Genie switched to the counter and Nitro stood back shaking his head at her smirking. This bitch was gone be his downfall, he already knew it. He was on for the challenge though.

Chapter 6

Let me catch a vibe, let's just take our time. Just relax your mind, and take it easy. Dani Leigh's Easy played softly through the speakers as Kill watched Kaylin throw her ass back onto his dick. She was riding his shit like it was a competition. Both of them knew it was her own insecurities that caused her to make it extra nasty every time she saw Kill.

Kill and Kaylin had known each other since highschool. What started as a friendship evolved to a fuckship. They were good enough to be friends and fuck. Kaylin made sure to play the fuck out of her role so nobody else could. She heard Kill when he told her he wasn't trying to be tied down. She respected it, to an extent.

If Kill wasn't ready, she wouldn't force it. But she would be first in line the minute he was taking applications. Kill's hands rounded her ass as he slapped it. Tugging lightly onto her 30 inches of brazillian body wave, her back arch. He sat up running his tongue up her back making her body shiver as a slight moan escaped her lips. Kill fisted her hair as he flipped her over, showing her what his jamaican waistline could do. "Akieeeeeel!" Grabbing her waist kill leaned into her and hit her with hard slow strokes. The strokes that made Kaylin want to spend her whole trip in the bedroom fucking and sucking him. Kaylin moans filled the penthouse suite. She couldn't think of a better way to spend her birthday, than in Vegas with Kill letting him kill her pussy.

Kill was serving dick three times a day for a week and she enjoyed every minute of it. He had her head in the clouds. Kaylin's body shuddered releasing her sexual tension onto his dick. Once Kill saw his dick coated sliding in and out of her he slid out. Kay swiftly flipped over taking him into her mouth whole. He watched as her head bobbed up and down as he grabbed her hair. The soft sensation of her fingers caressing his balls caused him to explode in her mouth.

Kay made sure to finish her drink, not allowing any of it to spill over as she stood up. She tiptoed and kissed Kill on the lips as she walked away. Kill had to stop himself from smacking her on the ass. "Where the fuck you learn that at?" Kill smirked as he followed her into the bathroom.

"One of my nigga's taught me that." Kaylin giggled, causing Kill's head to lean back.

"Well you sure enough got an A plus in sucking dick. You sure your niggas aint gay?" Kill cracked with a smirk causing Kaylin to burst into laughter. She swatted him with the wet rag popping his skin. The pinching pain caused him to raise his eyebrow. "Oh you wanna play with rags?" He taunted her playfully as he grabbed his own off the rack and ran water over it. Kaylin's eyes widened as she ran out of the bathroom laughing as he squeezed the water out and began rotating it.

"Akiel I'm sorry," She cried while pulling the comforter over her body hiding from him. Kill chuckled, he and Kaylin's relationship solely revolved around their comfortability. They were friends first and had set a solid foundation of friendship. It didn't matter that both of them were completely naked. For Kill sex was casual but the friendship was out of this world. Although Kay wasn't his girl she was definitely the main lady in his life. He snatched the cover back and she grabbed a pillow trying to cover herself.

"Get your punk ass up, don't start none it won't be none. What you tryna do today birthday baddie." He hyped her up knowing how much she loved birthdays. It was why he outdid himself every year. Every year since they'd graduate Kill celebrated Kay's life. She was the best friend he ever had and couldn't find in a nigga. Kay had turned out to be more solid than his day one niggas and it spoke volumes.

"I wanna go swimming with the dolphins, then skydiving,"

Kill shook his head causing her to giggle. Kaylin was adventurous and everytime they traveled she tried making Kill step out of his comfort. He was a hood nigga at heart, and hood niggas barely swam, yet enough with dolphins. "Imma take pictures of you swimming and shit, I'll jump out a plane with your crazy ass for sure."

"Nigga, you won't swim with dolphins but will jump your yellow ass out a plane? Backwards as hell."

"Man, missing an opportunity to push yo ass out a planc? Get the fuck outta here." He joked as he headed back into the bathroom and stepped into the shower.

A getaway was just what he needed. Kay's birthday came at the perfect time. Once he was done washing off he reentered the room Kay bypassed him ready for her turn with the hot shower. Kill watched as she closed the door and headed towards his bag that he'd packed, and pulled out a nicely wrapped box. He'd gone all out for Kay's birthday. He didn't mind. He had too much money, it was only an object for him. He dressed in a pair of Commes de Garçon sweats and a white T and converse. He waited for Kaylin to be done her hour-long shower. As she stepped out of the bathroom, the steam, and her natural glow caught Kill's attention. Kaylin was everything he wanted in a woman, and in the back of his mind, somewhere down the line if she stuck around long enough he could see them being. But not right now, and there was no time frame on it. The streets were grimey and if anyone knew that Kay was one of Kill's soft spots. She would be target practice. Kay was hood but she wasn't gangster, she could beat a bitch up but she wasn't pulling no triggers. In order for them to ever have a chance she needed to be able to protect herself at all times with him. Kill couldn't risk her life for his own selfish needs. Instead the friend zone they had was enough for him.

"Happy Birthday big head get dressed then open the shit." He told her as he looked at his diamond studded Rollie.

Once his phone began to ring he stepped out of the room and into the living room to talk while Kay got dressed.

"What's up?" Kill answered as Cher's name appeared on the screen.

"Hey, your uncle is in town and he wants you back home."

Kill was still a little thrown off that Cher was delivering the message instead of Rich or one of his other brothers. "Where's Rich?"

"Probably with the bitch he went to Jamaica with. You knew about her?" She asked him and Kill shook his head as if she could see him then spoke up.

"Nah, I didn't know about that,"

"I asked if you knew about her. But I guess that answers my question. I know you're gonna always take up for you brother, just don't fake the funk with me being phoney." Cher hung up. Kill was unsure what had just happened. His uncle Llanzo in town was never a good thing. Uncle Llanzo hated America and their strict laws. He only came when some shit was about to pop off or had already.

"I'm ready, now give me my damn gift." Kaylin playfully rolled her eyes as she grabbed the box quickly unwrapping it. When she opened the box Diamond studded double K necklace shined blinding her. It was so beautiful it took her breath away. Kaylin was grateful for Kill, he always went above and beyond.

"Killa Kay," He merged their names together as he put the necklace on her neck.

"I love it Akiel, wow. I guess you got a lil taste or whatever." She shrugged jokingly. Both of them laughed and Kill stuffed his hand in his pocket before he told Kaylin that his plans had changed.

"It's been a good three days."

"Your brothers calling?" Kaylin asked, already knowing the drill. Business was always first; it didn't matter the countries, time zone, or galaxy they were in, business was at the forefront of Kill's mind.

"Imma make it up to you when you get back home. I'll send a car to take you around while you out here. I'll come pick you up at the end of the week. Save the sky diving for me." He promised and a smile graced Kay's lips. Kill said what he would and wouldn't do and he made promises every time. It was his way of showing loyalty.

"You don't have to come back for me. Just send the jet and pick me up when I get back." She said, giving him a hug. She inhaled the scent of his Versace cologne enjoying it, one last time while they were on the island together. Kill wrapped his arm around her pulling her in kissing her forehead.

"Happy Birthday KK."

"Love you Kill, Be safe." With that Kill grabbed his bag, left stacks of money on the table and left out to catch his jet.

Chapter 7

Cher walked around Footprints making sure everything was in place for Rich's party, which was in a few hours. She needed everything on point. From the decorations to the security that was placed outside the doors, everything had to be perfect. Everything that she and Kill had come up with was slowly coming together. Her vision was coming to life and Kill paid every expense.

   She hurried into the kitchen to finish cooking for the evening ahead. There were oxtails falling from the bone, jerk chicken, rice and peas, rasta pasta, fried dumplings, roti escovitch and water crackers. All the food was just about done and just in time for her to go home and get ready for the party. Once Cher was satisfied with the casino theme decor done to the restaurant, she locked up and headed home.

   As she drove all she could think about was how grateful Rich would be. He wasn't big on birthdays but he was big on food and Cher made sure there was lots of it. With so much going on with them and the Mexicans a little celebration couldn't hurt. It was a celebration of his birthday, the day they met, and the day they were engaged. Rich's birthday held their most sentimental memories.

Through the trials and tribulations, her and Rich had been through so much but she loved that man with everything in her. Cher wasn't blind to the women he had on his dick. She knew she sat on the tip top of it. And as long as no one came to her as a woman she didn't go looking for them.

Pulling up to her house Cher admired her home that she shared with her family. This house brought her peace, it was her sanctuary. The only place her kids were able to run around, be free and have fun.

"Hey mama. You look so pretty today." Chasity called out the minute she stepped through the doors. Cher walked over to the couch sitting beside Chas who was watching TV. She fixed her hair out her face and gave her a warm smile.

"Thank you baby, your hair turned out nice. Don't get used to this though." Cher half joked. For Rich's birthday Cher let Chas get a Brazillian blowout because she didn't have time to do her hair. The length sat in the middle of her back and Cher was proud. Her magical hands could cook and grow hair.

"I love it mama."

"Okay, well I need you to start getting ready in like an hour. We have to make sure we're out of this house at seven o'clock so we can make it to the restaurant by seven thirty." Cher kissed her daughter on the forehead and headed to her bedroom.

When she saw that Rich wasn't there she instantly caught an attitude because knowing him, he was about to make them late. Cher's patience was running thin as she dialed his number and it went to voicemail. She thought about calling Kill, but they hadn't spoken since she summoned him from Vegas. It was going on a week. Instead she asked Chasity . "And where is the birthday man?"

"Daddy said he had to go out for a minute but he'll be back before six." Cher looked at her watch she seen it was only four o'clock and Rich had a hour in a half to be back home before she lost her fucking mind.

***

Across town Rich was laying in bed with Missy after an hour long sex session. He couldn't let the day go by without seeing his other woman.

"So what else do you have planned for today." Missy asked while laying on his chest tracing his tattoos with her fingers.

"My wife is throwing a party tonight! As much as mi don't want to go mi have to because she spent too much time planning it."

Missy rolled her eyes the minute the words came out of his mouth. She was sick of hearing those words. *His wife* The way he said it so casually made Missy's blood boil. Like he was constantly reminding her that he wasn't hers, but another woman's. "Yo wife, yo wife, yo wife! Fuck yo wife!" Missy stood up and put on her robe. Rich arose from the bed and began to put his clothes on because he knew she was about to start complaining. If it wasn't his wife, it was Missy. He couldn't win to lose. Someone would always be unhappy as long as he was happy.

"Just come to the party tonight. Be casual. Mi won't be with yuh but yuh can come if it'll make yuh happy!"

"I don't want you to just make me happy, I want to spend time with you! I know you married but damn can I get a little time!" Missy was livid, pissed off to be exact. The role of being a mistress was becoming too much for her to bare. Missy wanted more, she deserved more.

"Mi wife comes first! Mi will see you later!" Rich kissed Missy on the cheek and he walked out the house and headed home.

As soon as Rich walked in the house, Cher rolled her eyes at him. He'd left tornado Missy and came home to hurricane Cher. It was past six and Rich look and smelled cheap. "Your clothes are laid out on the bed, go take a shower and make it quick. Scrub good, because you smell like her." Cher scoffed, shaking her head. Her anger began to consume her because Rich's disrespect was blatant at this point. It was embarrassing and he walked around without a care in the world. She couldn't help the lone tear that fell from her eye. She wanted to tear his ass up with words but didn't want to spoil the evening she'd taken months to plan. Cher quickly wiped it away and walked to her vanity to do her makeup. Makeup would conceal her disdain, and cover up her sour mood.

"Yuh ready to go?" Rich asked as seven o'clock came around fast. They were a little behind schedule but Cher was just grateful they were finally making it out the house.

"Daddy you look nice." Chasity complimented him. She was sitting behind her daddy and ran her hand in his head playing with his dreads. She was a true daddy's girl.

"Tank yuh baby girl! Tonight we can watch movies like we always do on mi birthday. " Rich may not have been a good husband but when it came to being a father he was the best one for that job, no one could tell him different. He had the best mother he could ask for and it turned him into the great parent he was. His fathers parenting flaws taught Rich all the things not to do. After his parents had been murdered, Rich practiced being a good parent. He started with his brothers and when Chas came along she stole his heart and attention.

"Kamari told me about this scary movie on Netflix, that's what we'll watch." Chas beamed excited as sh e sat back in her seat. She was happy that Rich was keeping up with their birthday tradition even when Cher threw their plans for a loop. On Rich's birthday, they looked forward to two things. Good food and a good movie night.

***

"Yahso," Llanzo instructed his driver to stop as he pulled up to the DeLeon castle. He'd flown miles to keep his nephews alive. As much as he wanted to believe that Rich would take care of it, Llanzo didn't believe that his head was in the right place. So instead he'd flown to America to resolve whatever issues his hardheaded nephews had gotten themselves into.

His driver slowly drove up the driveway and Llanzo spotted all the mexican gang members with their guns in their hands. Like they were ready to shoot his car up. *What di fuck did these boys do?* Llanzo thought to himself. The driver rolled down the window and before he could press the buzzer the gates opened to him. It was clear, Alejandro DeLeon, head of the DeLeon mob had been waiting on his arrival.

"Gwan now," He instructed his driver knowing that there was a chance that they wouldn't make it out. There was no turning around even if he wanted to. They would be swiss cheese before the tires could do a u-turn. The hitters Llanzo had on the curbside of the street weren't enough. There were over forty men patrolling the house. They were outnumbered to say the least.

Llanzo let out a deep breath as they pulled up to the house. "If mi not out inna thirty minutes light dis muthafucka up." He ordered his driver with a devilish grin on his face.

As Llanzo stood at the front of the door he waited for the door to open. He didn't have to ring a bell to announce his presence. His presence was felt. He was the only motherfucker with a skin color and locs. The doors opened and Alejandro waved his gun at

Llanzo making him ease into the house. Alejandro's gun was pointed directly at Llanzo's head and he placed both his hands up. "Yu no want to chat like a man?"

Everything in Alejandro wanted to empty his clips into Llanzo's head, but he needed information out of him first. He had to know if his nephew Jose was still alive. That would be the only way Llanzo would be walking out of his castle was if it was in exchange for his nephew. "Fuck you, there is no chat. Where the fuck is my nephew?" Alejandro barked in Llanzo's face. He wanted to give Llanzo a reason to get bodied. But Llanzo had dealt with many men just like Alejandro, who laughed when they were up and cried when they were at the other end of the stick. Llanzo was unfazed by the five foot seven man. The seven inches he had him by he would use to kill Alejandro. Although making it out wasn't an option, he wouldn't be the only soul taken.

"Vado you know me, you know what I am capable of. Is Jose alive?"

"Alejandro, dis wasn't a part of di agreement. Wah mek yu cum to Atlanta?" Llanzo asked as he grilled Alejandro.

"Fuck the agreement! We made it twenty five years ago. You went back to Jamaica. The agreement was, as long as you are in Atlanta I stay out. You haven't been in Atlanta motherfucker. Now what the fuck happened to Jose." Alejandro screamed in Llanzo's face. He was testing Llanzo's patience and just as he was about to snap Alejandro's neck he heard his brother's voice. *Wen mi gon, you have fi tek care of mi pickney.*

"Wi have Jose but di only way yuh see him, is if mi get him." Llanzo lied as he dared Alejandro's ego to get in the way of the life of his family. If Llanzo said he was alive, Alejandro had to stand down.

Members of the DeLeon family stood around listening to the conversation between the two. Although many of them didn't believe Llanzo, including Alejandro. A few of them had hope. "Alejandro, deja que traiga a mi hijo" (Alejandro let him bring my son) His sister Selena said from behind him. She was one of the few with hope in her heart that the kid she'd carried for nine months was alive. She walked up to her brother putting her hand over his gun.

"You have ten minutes to bring me my son." Selena said to Llanzo as she removed the gun from Alejandro's hand and aimed it at his head. "Or you will bury your own family." She promised as she walked away. Llanzo and Alejandro grilled one another. Alejandro's insides boiled because Llanzo had said the right thing at the right time in front of the right people. His death was on pause. Deep down inside Alejandro knew that Jose was gone. If he wasn't Llanzo wouldn't have traveled across the world. He could tell Selena that same thing but the hope that Llanzo had instilled in her was the hope of a mother.

"Get the fuck out!" Alejandro barked as he opened the door. Llanzo wore a sly smirk on his face and it was the only other thing Alejandro needed him to do before Llanzo would feel his wrath.

"Mi gon see yu inna ten minutes." Llanzo smirked as he walked out of the DeLeon estate knowing he wouldn't be back. The only way he would be was with smoke coming from his AK.

"Enjoy your party," Alejandro called out to Llanzo, confusing him. His mind wondered what Alejandro was talking about as he got into his car.

"Get di fuck off dem property. We get ten minutes to get as far away as we can." Llanzo ordered the driver. It was all he needed to hear as he quickly made his way off the property.

Llanzo was sure they left tire marks on the DeLeon's driveway. He pulled out his phone and dialed Sonny's number. He was his youngest nephew and the one with the hardest head. Calling anyone else to relay the message to him that they were leaving the states, Sonny would give them trouble. Sonny was the type of nigga that needed to hear it from the horses mouth himself.

"Wah gwan Uncle," He answered. Llanzo could hear the loud music in his background.

"Mi no yu not at a party when you caused all this ruckus," Llanzo growled into the phone. He was livid at what he'd come to America too. He'd thought Rich could hold it down and raise his brothers but it was clear he was failing at it miserably.

"I'm at Rich's birthday party. I'm surprised you're not here Unc." As soon as the words came from Sonny's mouth Llanzo realized what Alejandro was talking about.

"Sonny listen to mi,"

RATATATATATATTAATTATTAT

Their piercing sound of an AK 47 pierced Llanzo's ears before he could say another word. His phone dropped from his hand as he yelled at his driver. "Drive di fucking car!

Chapter 8

"Yo the man of the hour is in the muh fucking house tonight. Everybody make some love for Rich muthafucking Vado. Happy birthday Nigga, you got a bottle of Clase Azul waiting for you." The DJ turned up as soon as Rich and his family walked through the door. He put two fingers to his temple and saluted the DJ to show some love.

"Happy birthday bro." Sonny grinned as he slapped fives with him pulling him into a bear hug. Out of all the brothers they were the most alike and it caused them to clash every time. It was like Sonny was consistently trying to prove to Rich that he was his equal. On every day except his birthday, this day was Rich's day. Nitro and Kill came over and showed him some love and Sonny handed him a shot.

"Take this shot with us nigga." Nitro ordered. He'd already had three shots and this was about to be his fourth. It had been so long since they were lit in their own territory since summer jam shit had been shaky. They tapped their glasses together and took their shots.

"Damn nigga, you old as fuck now. How it feel to be old ass dirt nigga?" Nitro threw his arm around Rich and all of them started walking to what Cher made the VIP section for tonight.

After a couple of shots, The Vado brothers were feeling good and having a great time. The DJ played the hottest hits. His wife was happy, his kids were happy and his brothers were happy. Rich's heart was full to capacity. His peripheral vision caught Missy easing her way into the restaurant. He'd snuck her name on the guest list when Cher was in the back getting the food together. Missy looked good as fuck, she came dressed in a all black Prada dress and some red and black red bottom heels.

"Aye, I'm about to go make my rounds and talk to my guest. Don't let this fool get drunker than he already is." Rich put his hands on Nitro's shoulder, then walked away.

"Aye, man happy birthday."

"My nigga you another year older."

"Yo wife put her foot in this food." Everybody was trying to stop Rich to have a conversation with him but his mind was only on Missy. Just that quick she stole his attention and he couldn't help but go to her. Most men would have been sick to see their wife and mistress in the same room, but Rich he liked a challenge.

"Daddy come over here so we can get our picture taken." Chasity grabbed Rich's hand and pulled him towards the photobooth that Cher rented. "Let's get mommy too, so we can take a family picture." Although Rich wanted to go and find Missy, his daughter came first.

Missy looked on with envy as she watched Rich take pictures with his family. The family she wanted desperately. She wanted Cher to drop dead somewhere, even though that was wishful thinking. Downing her glass of wine, Missy made a bold move and walked over to Rich and Cher.

"Happy Birthday Badrick," She waltzed over to him with seduction in her voice. "Do you mind if I get a picture with you too? You're the boss in Atlanta."

Cher was a lot of things but stupid she wasn't. As any woman would, she looked Missy from head to toe and she peeped the tattoo on her right tittie that said Rich. Missy knew exactly what she was looking at and smirked at her.

"Bitch, if you don't ge-" Before Cher could get her words out shots rang out.

RATATATATATAT TAT TAT TAT TAT

Rich yanked Cher to the ground as she tried to grab her kids. "Stay down!!" Rich screamed at her. Rich looked for his brothers as bodies began to drop. The shots were deafening and blood covered the floor. It was a bloodbath and he needed to make sure none of his blood had been spilled. When he saw Akiel tuck Enoch under his body, and Nitro lying over Legend, he looked around to set his eyes on the last two of his blood then he could let out a sigh of relief.

"Rich, where's Chasity?!" Cher screamed over the loud shots. The sound of the kids crying filled the ear along with everyone's fears. Nobody thought they'd be making it out of there alive. Rich had lived 39 years and if he died today he would be okay as long as his family was good. "Find my baby!!" Cher cried hysterically as the shots continued.

POW POW POW POW POW

The sound of shots still ringing tortured guests. Some were traumatized, paranoid, and scared straight. After about five minutes the gunshots stopped and everyone laid on the floor scared to get up.

Scared that there were more bullets to come. But as everyone stayed down Sonny finally came into sight and everyone looked at him with sorrow filled eyes.

"Rich, Cher." He called out almost unable to speak. A limp Chasity laid in his hands. Cher quickly jumped to her feet and looked on in horror as she watched Sonny carry her baby towards them. Chasity was gone, Cher knew it before even touching her. But Rich was in denial.

"Cum on baby, we ave to tek Chas tu di hospital. Dey ave to save mi Chasity ." Rich's voice cracked as he grabbed Chasity from Sonny. He headed out the door with his baby girl in his arms hoping and praying that she had another life to live.

Cher, Kill, Nitro, and Sonny followed with the kids in tow as all the other guests began making a run for it, not wanting to be a part of any of the other mess that was sure to come. Everyone there knew that once you came for the Vado family then the Vado family was sure to come back ten times harder. Missy stood up and watched the Vado's all leave the restaurant. It was then she realized that she was the outsider and would always be. Rich and Cher had their own life built together and his need to protect his wife over her pissed

Missy off to the fullest. She was angry and hurt all in one. Being the side chick wasn't an option any more. She wanted to be the head bitch in charge and she was coming for that spot.

Chapter 8

"Wi need a muthafucking doctor." Rich ran in the hospital with a limp Chasity in his arm. His baby wasn't breathing and the doctors needed to do everything in their power to help Chas or he was blowing this whole damn hospital up. A team of doctors and nurses came rushing towards him when his family came through the doors.

"Sir, you have to let her go, let me do my job." A doctor took Chasity out of his arms and put her on a gurney.

"Where are you taking her. Where the fuck is he taking my baby." Cher fell to her knees crying.

"What's the Patient's name?" A nurse walked over to Rich. But Rich's mind was in a completely different world. His baby girl had been shot and everybody would pay. He couldn't talk, think or speak. The only thing he wanted to hear was Chasity was gonna be okay.

"Her name is Chasity Vado." Cher finally calmed herself down and went to stand next to Rich. All the questions the nurse asked Cher answered them while Nitro, Kill and Sonny were talking.

"Rich what the fuck is taking them so long. Where the fuck is my baby at." Cher fussed an hour later. They were still sitting in the waiting room with no update and she'd exuded her patience.

"Family of Chasity Vado?" A doctor finally came out with blood on his white coat.

"Yes, yes, that's us." Cher was the first one up and in the doctor face while Rich stood behind her.

"Mrs. Vado, I'm sorry to inform you but Chasity didn't make it. Chasity was shot eight times total. Once in the four in her back, once in the chest, twice in the stomach and once in the arm. We tried everything to bring her little body back to life but the bullets to her back and stomach were too much for her to bear. I am so sorry for your loss, I'm going to have a nurse take you back to her room to see her one last time before we take her away. Again Mr and Mrs Vado, I am so sorry for your loss." The doctor turned to walk away and Sonny turned punching the wall.

"Fuck man, Fuck. My fucking niece." Sonny barked. His guilt that he hadn't gotten to her in time ate at him. Nitro and Kill had gotten to Legend and Enoch, and he had one job which was to protect his niece. He had failed her. By the time he'd grabbed Chas she was already limp. He fell to the floor, being the most vulnerable he'd ever been in public. Nitro and Kill nudged Rich towards his wife letting him know that they had Sonny.

Cher was in a daze looking loss as Rich came over and tried to hug her. The loss of her daughter took everything out of her. She couldn't scream, cry, or feel anything. She was just stuck. *My baby is gone.* Processing the words in her mind was a mental beat down.

"This is all on you, if you weren't too busy entertaining that bitch at your party my daughter would still be here. Don't fucking touch me Rich, don't say shit else to me. This time, this Vado shit has gone too far. Fuck you Rich, Fuck you." Cher fell to the floor again and Kill walked over picking her up. He'd heard her words, everyone did and he could tell from the look on Rich's face, Cher's words stuck. She'd so quickly placed the blame on him when he hadn't even been able to grasp the reality that his first born was gone.

"If you're ready I can take you back to see your baby now." A nurse came and got the family. Kill, Sonny and Nitro went first so they could say their goodbyes. Sonny took it the hardest, seeing as though he'd failed to protect her. He felt small, like a failure, like a motherfucking boy and it ate at his conscience. After kissing Chasity goodbye, they all walked out the room and Cher and Rich entered.

"I'm right outside the room bro." Kill put his hand on Rich's shoulder for support and Rich nodded at him.

Walking into the room and seeing Chasity laid on the bed in her blood not breathing set Cher on a brink to insanity.

"My baby, Mama loves you so much Chas. I'm so sorry. Mommy can't believe this happened to you. Chasity please wake up for mama." Cher cried as her eyes leaked like a faucet and her heart broke into a million pieces. She climbed into the bed with Chasity not caring that she was getting her four thousand dollar dress bloody. She just wanted to be near her baby. Cher buried her face in Chasity neck and she cried the hardest she ever cried before. The love between a daughter and a mother could never compare to anything else. This was her baby, her heart, her twin, her introduction to motherhood. The baby who gave Cher a reason to live. How was Cher going to live without her. Rich heart broke a little more with each cry that Cher let out. What was even harder for him was that Cher blamed him. He couldn't touch his wife in their time of need, because she hated him. Was this really his fault?

Unable to watch Cher mourn much longer he stepped out the room and instructed Kill to take her home. Rich wanted to be with his wife but he needed time with Chasity before he left this hospital.

"Come on sis." Kill went to grab Cher and she went crazy.

"NO, NO. I'M NOT LEAVING MY BABY HERE. SHE NEEDS ME KILL, SHE NEEDS ME. PLEASE DON'T MAKE ME LEAVE." She wailed like a child. Snot covered her face as her eyes were puffy from crying.

"Pick her up and take her." Rich ordered again knowing that his wife would live in the hospital with Chas if they let her. Doing as his brother said, Kill picked Cher up and carried her out the room while she called Rich everything but a child of God. Her baby was gone and her heart was ripped out her chest.

Once Cher's curses could no longer be heard, Rich sat beside Chasity's bed and allowed his tears to fall freely. "Baby girl, what mi going tuh do without yuh? mi so sorry, mi should have been paying more attention to yuh. Yuh are still mi heart in human form. Mi so fucking sorry Chasity." Laying his head on Chasity 's bed by her side he cried. Rich had let down every guard he'd ever had as he felt like a failure. He didn't deserve to live. He would switch with her if it was possible. He lightly banged his head on the tail of her bed as his angst took over.

Rich stayed in sorrow until the doctors told him it was time to let her go. He kissed his baby girl on the cheek, and walked out feeling empty and ready for revenge.

***

The car ride to Rich's home made Kill uneasy. Cher's cries taunted him, they were tears of a mother. Tears that none of them could compare to, it would be selfish to cry with her in that moment. Today was a sad day in the Vado family, but Cher's pain superseded everyone else's in Kill's eyes. He pulled up to their home and climbed out the car grabbing a sleeping Legend from his carseat as Cher Xs picked up a sleeping Enoch. Cher's silence stunned Kill. Cher was a great mother. She would silence her tears to stop her kids from seeing them. Not wanting to scare them. Cher's heart was so heavy that it made her weak. The weight of her baby made tears fill her eyes. She remembered when Chas was just as small. Reality slapped her in the face as she laid Enoch in his bed.

She hadn't even realized that she'd walked all the way to the room. Cher had blacked out so easily that it scared her. She put her hand over her mouth to muffle her cries and rushed out the room. She closed the door behind her and walked down the stairs taking a seat beside Kill. She didn't have any words, nothing could come from her mouth except cries. "Are you gonna be okay?" Kill asked genuinely concerned as he turned to her. Cher nodded her head as tears fell from her eyes. The face and body movement weren't adding up and Kill knew there was no way he could leave her. Not until Rich came in. Kill's heart softened as he thought of his brother and the thoughts that had been going through his head. Everyone reacted to death differently and Rich's reaction was making a blood bath. He would die killing off Mexicans whether they were related to the DeLeon or not.

Cher wiped her tears and shrugged. "Will I ever be okay? How am I supposed to live like this Kill. She's my first baby, my only baby girl! She made me a mom and now she's just gone!" She asked a rhetorical question. She wanted to know if pain like this lasted forever. The loss of a child was different from any pain. One that crippled and kill anyone it consumed. This was a pain she wouldn't wish on anyone, not even her worst enemy. The numb feeling in her heart was unbearable. Living seemed like it was too good for her, why was she still on this earth and her daughter was not. Children were supposed to outlive their parents and here she was about to bury her first child.

"Tonight you'll be okay, cause I'm not going anywhere." Kill said standing up putting his hand out for her. Cher was thankful that Kill was deciding to stay rather than her asking. She needed someone, anyone that wasn't Rich. Cher couldn't stand the sight of him right now and she didn't trust herself alone. She gave Kill a weak smile and placed her hand in his. He led her to the living room and Cher sat on the couch looking at the black TV screen.

Kill's sympathy for her spilled over as he watched her black out into another world of her own as he turned the TV on. He grabbed the two of them a glass and a bottle of Hennessy and sat beside her. "Yo, what you tryna watch?" He asked, slicing Cher's thoughts in half. He needed to get her mind off Chas.

"Nothing, I just can't right now. I don't understand Kill, everything happened so fast. She was there then she wasn't. There was so much blood coming from her." Cher ranted as her breathing got heavy. She was living in a nightmare and it was haunting her.

"Cher we gon get them niggas back. That's my word to you, I'll bring the nigga head to you on a plate ma." Kill could see the pain in Cher's eyes and it upset him. He didn't have any kids, so he didn't know exactly how Cher was feeling. If he could put his hands in hers and take all her pain away that would be exactly what he would do. He'd do it in a heartbeat if that meant she would be okay.

Cher could hear Kill's voice weak as it cracked. He'd lost his niece and was putting own feelings at the back burner to be there for her. Cher tried pulling herself together, Kill had done enough of helping her. She needed to give a little more effort. *I have my whole life to grieve.* She thought to herself as she wiped her tears and grabbed the bottle of Hennessy. Holding in her tears was becoming too much and she just needed the pain to go away. She placed the bottle to her lip gulping, and gulping, and as she was about to continue Kill grabbed the bottle from her. Cher's face was twisted in an ugly form making Kill chuckle.

"You done grew hair on your chest after that." He tried lightening up the room, but Cher was back in her daze. She laid her head onto Kills shoulders and he allowed her.

"I really don't want you to leave but I don't really want to talk Akiel. My heart is too heavy to try and do anything else but try and register what happened."

"I told you I'm not going nowhere. But can we at least have music on? This silence ain't good at a time like this. Shit is making a nigga feel crazy."

Cher cracked a small smile realizing the silence was filled with tension from both of their pain and neither of them could fix it. But music could. She picked up her phone and put on Good Days by SZA. Cher's head never left Kill's shoulder and he just sat up with his head laid back onto the couch. This time the silence between them became comfortable as they both cried silent tears not wanting to be selfish to the other. Kill was grateful that Cher never looked up, he never wanted anyone to see him cry. His reasoning for being here was to be strong for Cher, but the pain of losing his niece was weighing down on him. Chasity was the glue that held the family together. The first Vado baby girl that had been brought home. The one that kept smiles on everyone's face. Kill couldn't get the thoughts of her out of his head.

Hours went by and Cher's playlist and Hennessy had them slumped. Sonny entered to the awkward visual of Kill sleep with his arms across his chest while it was apparent Cher's head had fallen into his lap. "Akiel," He nudged and Kill woke up instantly confused. He was out in dreamland and when he woke up he almost forgot that he was still at Rich's home. Until he looked at Sonny's accused face, Kill finally looked down and saw Cher. He shook his head while slowly moving her off of him and laying her fully on the couch.

Kill stretched his bones and met Sonny at the door. They locked up and before Kill stepped into his car Sonny leaned over the roof of his own with one foot in his car. "You don't need me to tell you that y'all looked crazy right."

"I don't bro, I already seen it for myself. It won't happen again." Kill answered as he climbed into his car and sped off his brother's property. Cher stayed on his mind and Sonny bringing up his point of view didn't make anything better. Their friendship was feeling more like a soul tie when their souls hadn't been entangled. Being around Cher just felt so right, Kill couldn't understand why Rich didn't do right. But it wasn't for him to understand. Kill just put it in his mental to put space between him and Cher. If Sonny's wild ass had gotten the wrong impression anyone would.

Chapter 9

Red means dead. Rich thought to himself as he sat on the outside of the DeLeon Estate. All he could see was red. Chas's blood was engraved in his mind, and at the forefront of his eyelid. All he could think was death, his eyes hawked the gate waiting on it to open. Waiting on someone to come out so they could settle the score. He was ready to make the DeLeon family extinct. They deserved it. He was a broken father and needed to get some type of retribution for his daughter to feel like he hadn't failed her. Seeing her on the hospital bed lifeless had done something to him. It had dismantled him, making him less of a man. *Why couldn't I take that shot for her.*

"Badrick, wi ah go get ours." Llanzo reassured Rich as he put his hand onto his shoulder. He could feel Rich's deadly spirit, ready to curl a trigger and take a couple lives. Llanzo was down to ride with his nephew because their blood had been spilled. The loss of Chasity made Llanzo's stomach hollow. His great niece had yet to experience her life to its full potential. The DeLeon's had violated. Broke two street codes in one. No women and children were to get touched. Chasity was two in one and Llanzo knew it was only right to avenge her death. The only thing Llanzo and Rich weren't on the same page about was going in blindly, guns blazing. The sweat that poured from Rich's forehead, his bloodshot eyes, and tight grip on his gun told Llanzo Rich was ready to end it all; his rage was getting the best of him and Llanzo couldn't allow it to be the death of him. "Luk fi mi," he demanded Rich while turning his chin towards him.

Tears sat at the brim of Rich's eyes. He refused to let them fall always wanting to appear strong to his uncle. He'd been raised by two strong men, his father and Llanzo. They'd taught Rich everything he needed to know about being a man. And although Rich took after his father more than his uncle, the weight Llanzo held in his life remained the same. "Right now, yuh don have fi be strong. That's wah I'm here fi. I've dealt wid di DeLeon's before. Guns blazing won't tek dem out. You kill one ten more jump out di clown car. Dey multiply." Llanzo explained. He needed Rich to hear his words and understand them. He needed to clear his mind, he'd been like Rich once. When he'd lost his brother in the last war between the two families. One thing Llanzo had learned was the DeLeon's were strategic at all times. They had too much money and manpower and after years of hating them Llanzo knew the only way to take them out was to hit them where it hurt. "Wi ave fi hit dem weh fi hurt. Wi tek dem products, dem funds, den dem lives but first wi need leverage,"

"Mih dawta is gone. She's nuh coming back. Mih first born. Dem have tuh pay! Mih don't care bout di ten that's coming, as long as mih get one, mih have enough! Rich couldn't hold it anymore, his tears started to fall and it didn't care. He wanted them dead and he wanted them dead now. Anyone with the last name DeLeon. He wanted their bodies ripped into shreds and he wanted them dead as of yesterday.

"Well nuh care bout yuh, mih don't want yuh dying. I already lost mi bredda and yuh mada, mih don't wanna lose my nephew tuh. I put yuh in charge for a reason Rich. Tink smart." The sound of Chasity 's spirit praising took over the car as the gates to the DeLeon mansion finally opened. "Whoeva sed God not real, neva believe inna him tuh begin wid. Dat right there is di DeLeon princess. She worth more dan gold."

Llanzo and Rich eyes both stayed trained on Genesis DeLeon as she pulled out from the gates. Two cars pulled out after her following her and Llanzo rubbed his hands together. This was too easy. For once he felt like he was a step ahead of the Alejandro.

Alejandro had given him the kiss of death when he left from his house and Llanzo was ready to return it. He rolled down his window and used two fingers to pointing them forward to summon his men to follow her.

"Mi guh kill dat bitch!" Rich growled as Llanzo slowly pulled off the hidden curb and followed.

"Yuh wi get yuh fun nephew. Let's grab di bitch when she get far enough and make dem pay." He wanted to wait until there was enough distance between Genie and her home before they decided to extract her.

Ten minutes from the DeLeon home was too much for Rich and he couldn't wait any longer. He slowly rolled down his window and slid out the window aiming his AK47 at Genie's Calvary.

Tat tat tat tat tat attat

Play time was over, Rich's patience had turned to insanity. He needed to see blood. Someone's blood other than Chas's. Llanzo quickly stopped the car and grabbed his semi-automatic as well and began blasting alongside his nephews and his shooters. Once again blood was being spilled between the DeLeon mob and Vado gang and this time Vado had come prepared.

Genie sat in her car with complete panic in her heart but she knew better. Her father had taught her better. He'd taught her how to fight for her life whenever he wasn't around and the sound of the bullets tearing through the air, bodies dropping, glass breaking, she knew her time to save herself was limited. She quickly grabbed her 9mm and slid out of her car shooting in the direction where the bullets took out her guards. All of her men laid on the floor in pools of their own blood. Genies mind was conflicted between fight or flight. She was outnumbered, but she was also blocked in and couldn't go anywhere.

POW POW

She dropped two of the shooters from Vado gang. She ducked behind her car as bullets flew towards her. She wasn't ready to die, but she was prepared to, if it meant fighting for her life. Once the bullets stopped Genie stood again, stepping in front of her car she knew it was do or die. Feeling like the woman Scarface, she was ready. She didn't give a fuck, if she was going to die she was going to die a bad bitch. Alejandro didn't raise a weak bitch, she was going to die making him proud.

POW

A bullet went through her right shoulder causing her to stumble back and her gun to fall from her hand. Genie tried to get to the gun but the pain was unbearable. She'd never felt anything like it. The burning sensation slowly took over her entire arm. Her heart raced and fear consumed her as blood began to seep through her shirt.

POW

"Ahhhhhh" Genie cried as another shot went through her legs. Tears filled her eyes as she realized that this was it. Her life span stopped at twenty one. No kids, no husband. Her life was over. She had gotten a taste of the good life and now her life was being taken as a consequence from him. Fear caused her life to flash before her eyes, she thought about all the wrong she had done in her life. All the people she had betrayed and the people she uplifted. This wasn't the way she thought she would die. Genie knew she shouldn't have but she thought of Nitro and the time they'd spent together. She wanted to fight for her life but the pain in her shoulder and leg was making it impossible. She did a silent prayer as footsteps neared her. Trying to think of a way to save herself, she couldn't. Her mind was empty, her guns were too far and the pain she was in, there wasn't a word to describe it. She was ready and anticipating the last shot to take her out but it never came.

"Mih bout tuh have fun wit tis bitch, Alejandro's princess bout tuh be meat fa mih damn dogs."

"Yuh no have any dogs nephew." Llanzo laughed at his nephew even though he knew it was a serious moment. He kept his eyes on Genie so she would try no slick shit.

"I'm a get one."

"Que te jordan! Mi padre u mi hermano se fueron a buscarte y matarte! Outa Cabron!(Fuck you! My daddy and brother gone find you and kill you! Rot in hell bitch.)
A pistol to her head knocked her lights out.

"Get tis bitch a take her tuh our hidden spot." Rich told his gang. It was taking everything in him not to kill her and leave her on the side of the road. He didnt give a fuck about anything but making her pay for what her bitch ass family did. If Llanzo wasn't with him, he would have done just that. Left the DeLeon princess slumped just like they'd done his Vado princess.

Chapter 10

Nitro sat in his car waiting on Genie to hit him back up. They were supposed to be meeting at the skating rink again. Picking up his phone he dialed Genie's number again and her phone went straight to voicemail.

Where the hell is shorty at? Nitro dialed again and got the same results. Impatient, he went over to the concession stand and grabbed him something to drink since Genie was taking her sweet ole time. Nitro wondered what in the hell he did to Genie. He wondered if the Imani situation had run her away but quickly pushed that to the back of his mind. *I blew shorty back out twice after that, so nah.* He waited a few more minutes before shrugging and leaving the rink.

"Fuck it her loss. As good as the pussy was, I aint bouta stalk her." He said to himself feeling like a clown as he sat in his car talking to himself. He laughed and shrugged it off.

Nitro's phone began ringing as he was about to pull into Mcdonald's parking lot. Llanzo's name appeared on the screen and he instantly answered.

"Wassup unc." Nitro parked his car so he could talk to his uncle.

"Denetro, meet us at di basement. Come around back when you get here."

Some shit about to pop off. He thought to himself. With the family he was dealt with, his adrenaline was always rushing, there was always some shit they were in and after Chas's death he wasn't surprised to be getting the call he got. They believe in the law of retaliation. An eye for an eye. Or in their case, a kid for a kid. Rubbing his hands together he pulled off getting straight on the highway to go handle business.

"Yo siri, play Mo3 And I"

On the block from nine to five we getting paper in the middle of the jungle with that burner on me.

Nitro was feeling his music as he did ninety on the highway to get to his family. The bloodbath had just started. The war had spiraled and nobody was off limits. Once he pulled up he hopped out the car and Sonny met him in the stairway energized, like he'd just finished drinking an energy drink.

"Bro we finally got one of them damn DeLeon's. You ain't gonna believe this shit, we been waiting on yo ass. Where the hell you been at?"

"That's a story for another day. Let's send them niggas another message." Nitro was hype and ready to hurt somebody, especially since Genie had played him the way she did. His ego had been slightly bruised and he was ready to take it out on a motherfucker who deserved it.

He entered the basement thinking about everything that he was about to do to the DeLeon family. "Nitro bout time you joined the fun." Kill smirked and dapped his brother.

Slowly lifting her head, when Genie and Nitro's eyes connected a flame lit behind her eyes. Rage, confusion, and hatred all filled her at once. She knew this couldn't be the same Nitro she was spending all her time with, it couldn't have been. He'd played her. Genie felt stupid, betrayed, and most of all for the first time since she met him Nitro broke her heart. *Was this his plan all along. How long has he been plotting on me?*

"She's a DeLeon?" Nitro asked the only question that plagued his mind. He saw the hate, and the rage behind her eyelids.

This bitch been plotting the whole time? He was in utter disbelief. All the feelings Nitro thought he had for Genie went out the window. Nitro was furious because he didn't understand how he didnt know who Genie was. Nothing in his mind believed that things were a coincidence. He'd seen her at The Underground and she'd had him on her radar the entire time. Genie had to know who he was, and now that Nitro knew who she was he wondered if her standing him up was good or bad.

Genie had so many thoughts running through her mind. *How the fuck did I fall for a night that's setting me up?* It was like her entire world was standing still. She'd fallen for him. Hard, and there was no chance they could ever be. *I should've known he was a fuck nigga. A fucking snake.* Trying her hardest not to let the tears fall from her eyes she spat blood out her mouth and it landed right by Nitro shoes.

"There ain't shit you could do to me to make me talk! I'm a fucking DeLeon. Once my daddy catches you, straight headshots for everyone." Genie pushed her feelings to the side and put on her game face.

"Shut di fuk up." Rich slapped Genie with all his might and Genie's head turned from impact. The blow had been so hard she felt her neck pull a muscle. Rich's hurt and anger was consuming him, his baby girl was gone and he was ready to take it out on everybody. "Yuh and yuh family gone pay." Genie held her tears. Refusing to let them fall, she was the only woman in a room full of men. The intimidation didn't work on her. She was a thoroughbred. She could feel the toxic energy in the room from everyone's mind. Everyone had one thing in their mind, murder.

"Let's go talk before wi kill dis bitch." Llanzo walked out the room and his nephews followed.

"So what we gone do with her." Nitro was the first to speak as soon as they were out of the room.

"We gone collect ransom, call the DeLeons and tell them they can get proof of life if they send five million. I don't want nothing less." Llanzo was ready to get rid of these Mexicans once and for all. They had proven that they weren't worthy of being on this earth.

"We ain't giving di bitch back." Rich slammed his hand on the table. His uncle was saying nothing that he wanted to hear. He wanted to hear the sound of a bullet going in Genie's skull to even the playing field.

"Women off limits Rich, you know that." Kill finally spoke.

"That rule went out when mih daughter was killed. Mih want her dead, after wi get this money." As Rich rose from the table, Llanzo's phone rang and they all looked at each other.

"Tawk tuh me." Llanzo put the phone on speaker and put it in the middle of the table so they all could hear.

"Where the fuck is my daughter, you think we killed yo niece. If I don't get my daughter back I'm taking your whole family out!" Alejandro was yelling in the phone like he would come through it any minute.

"Mih don't tink yuh in the position to make demands. Yuh give mih five million and yuh get proof dat yuh daughter is still alive. Mih will even let yuh facetime her. If yuh don't get mih, mih money than she's good as dead." Llanzo was cold, he didnt give a fuck. His niece was gone and Alejandro was gone pay with his daughter's life.

"How do I know she's alive."

"Dih only way to know is to have five mill sent to the account that's coming to yuh phone now."

Kill pulled out his burner phone and sent the account number to Alejandro. "Yuh ave twenty four hours." Llanzo hung up and exited the basement. Genie was their hostage until Alejandro put her out her misery. How soon they ended it all depended on if Alejandro obliged with his rules.

***

A shot from the bottle of black Hennessy caused Sonny's chest to burn as he sat back and thought about his niece. This was his first real loss that was close to home and he didn't know how to cope with the shit. The Henny in this system until he passed out did the trick most of the time. That shit was hurting him to the core and all he wanted to do was drink his pain away. Chasity was gone and his soul was burdened. He took blame for it all internally. The war had occurred because of his behavior and so fast, shit had gone from bad to worst.

"Why you over here looking like you lost yo best friend." Troi entered his section and handed him a bottle of water.

"Ma, you don't know the half." Sonny shook his head as he took another shot. His eyes watered but he didn't let his tears fall.

"Look at me." Troi took a seat across from Sonny and took the henny bottle placing it behind her as she opened the bottle of water and passed it to him. She'd spotted him drinking liquor like a fish and knew if Sonny didn't have some water his lungs would collapse. He'd been in the underground for hours and hadn't bothered Troi. It wasn't like him and although she'd waited two hours to approach him, she'd been worried about him.

"My niece was killed, and that shit has my mind blown. A nigga heart is weary. The soul I didn't even know I had, feel like it's weighing on my chest."

"It sounds like you need a minute to recuperate. To digest what's going on, and to try to process mourning."

"Nah, I ain't trying to mourn. I just wanna put bodies in the dirt, but right now that's not my call. So I gotta sit back like a bitch. Sitting on my hands without letting my muzzle go." Sonny was opening up to Troi. He was unsure if it was liquid courage or what but Troi made him comfortable. They'd spent enough time at the bar entertaining one another and he was open to calling her a friend.

"Sonny, you better than that. The game has always been the same, the rules just apply differently. You get to decide what your next move is and if it's your best move." Troi's words silenced him. She needed him to think of the consequences of his action. His urge to retaliate would never end the war.

"Leave with me tonight."

"I will, let me finish some more of the shift out and we can get out of here. I'll let you know when I'm ready to go so you can meet me out front. I'm taking this Henny bottle with me. Sober up." Winking at him Troi was already thinking of ways to help him tonight. Sonny wasn't processing his feelings the proper way. He was so full of rage that he was unsure how to feel anything other than it. She'd seen him wringing his hands along with twisting his dreads. His nerves were sending him over the edge. Troi was smitten by Sonny, and his change in attitude worried her. His always flirtatious and playful behavior had done a complete 360 and for the many times he'd put a smile on her face she wanted to return the favor.

Troi finished the rest of her rounds while Sonny tried sobering up in his section. The thought of Troi going home with him had lightened his pain a little. Someone to talk to so he didn't drive himself crazy in his head. Every time he'd offered to take Troi home she'd declined his offer. But today she'd finally given in. Sonny had her worried.

"Meet me out front." Troi finally let Sonny know two hours later. "I'll follow you,"

Sonny's face wore a skeptical look and Troi rolled her eyes and scoffed. Sonny's hesitance spoke volumes and she wasn't into applying pressure on niggas. He had been the one who invited her to his home and now he was hesitating. That was enough for Troi to walk away.

"Troi chill, I'm sorry. A nigga mind just clouded. I don't know who to trust."

"I'm not after you. Just trying to help. How about you drive my car." She told him while tossing him the car keys. Sonny caught them mid air and gave her a wink.

"I dont have to worry about no petty ass girl coming to fuck up my car?" Troi half-joked as they pulled up to his home.

Sonny's house impressed Troi as she slipped her shoes off when she entered. It was fully furnished and resembled a family home rather than a bachelor pad.

"Nah, believe me or not you the first woman at my house. A nigga too reckless, I don't put shit past these bitches. This my kingdom, where I rest my head. Not too many people can say they've been here." He grabbed a bottle of Henny and two glasses and took a seat on the couch.

Troi trailed behind him and took a seat at the other end of the couch. "Come here why you way over there." He waved her over. Troi walked over to Sonny and he pulled her down onto his lap. He and Troi had been playing a fun game of cat and mouse and he was the cat, and finally caught the mouse. "Yo hair clean?" He asked as he sat up and placed his hand in her dreaded scalp twisting her hair instead of his own. Her back length dreads hung loosely over her shoulders making their hair identical.

"Boy don't play with me." She giggled as she closed her eyes. The feeling of Sonny softly retwisting her hair made her entire body shudder. There was something about little intimate shit from a hood nigga. Especially Sonny. Troi had never seen him be gentle. She'd seen him come and go with plenty of bitches handling them roughly in the clubs. She hadn't known that he was capable of being gentle. Troi stood from his grasp already beginning to feel herself getting intoxicated by their slight contact. "I need to take a shower, come show me where it's at." She stood over him reaching her hand out waiting on him to grab it. Sonny stood up towering her.

"Don't stand over me unless you riding me. Come on." He told her seriously. Troi was unlike any other women he met. She was older than him by four years, and she carried herself different from everyone else he'd been around. She played games, the type that gave him a challenge and he loved that shit. Sonny led her to the bathroom and all it's toiletries. For a nigga that lived alone and didn't invite women over, he had enough spare everything to make Troi comfortable.

Sonny occupied himself at the bar as Troi got herself together. It was like if she wasn't in his face, a drink was. He had two options to numb his feelings and it was Troi, or a drink. He poured her a glass of henny and shook off his emotions before he reentered his master bedroom. He entered the bathroom and he stopped in his tracks as he watched Troi wash her body through the shower glass. She was like a work of art. Her beautiful honey skin complexion glistened with every drop of water that covered her. Her natural curves hypnotized him. The stretch marks, and cellulite turned him on more than he'd ever been. Most women he fucked with had their body done. They had big ass, no waist, nice titties. But Troi was different; her ass had his full attention. She was perfect naked and his dick couldn't control itself as he stared on.

Feeling his eyes on her, Troi looked out the glass and continued washing her body while locking her eyes with his. *You want a show? Imma give you one.*
Troi slowly bent down washing her legs and making sure Sonny got a full view of her ass. He wanted her so bad that it made her want to give herself to him. A woman of her caliber Sonny had never had. She was one that was comfortable with the word no. She'd fought off her urge for Sonny for so long but the bulge in his pants made Troi want to take him for a spin. "Come in," she told him as curved her index finger.

Her words were like music to his ear, Sonny wasted no time stripping down. He tied his dreads up and stepped into the shower. He turned her around as he kissed her back. He used his index finger to play with her throbbing clit and she let out a small moan as the palm of her hands rested on the shower wall. Sonny's hands caressed her love box like it was a dick. Like he'd learned which spot made a woman's back arch vs what spot made her toe curls.

"Damn baby, that shit tight as fuck. All this for me." Kissing her neck he continued to tease her. Troi removed his hand and spun around facing him. As much as she had held back from Sonny she wanted him, every single part of him.

"It tastes even better baby," she whispered in his ear and Sonny almost hesitated for a second time. He wasn't an eater. At least he hadn't been before Troi. Her words caused him to kneel under her like she was his queen. He threw her thigh over his shoulder and licked over her budding rose. Troi fisted his wet dreads and rubbed her cat all over his face. "Suck my fucking clit boy," she moaned. Sonny's lips and tongue did all the work his hand usually did with women. Troi wasn't into a half assed orgasm. She wanted the full experience and as she grinded onto Sonny's face she smirked. *This pussy gon fuck his life up.* She thought and as soon as he entered his fingers into her Troi's eyes squeezed shut. Sonny had hit the jackpot.

He played with her jewel while sucking on her clit and the combo caused Troi to cum all over his face.

Not one to be out done Troi turned to face Sonny and dropped down to her knees. She look into his eyes, as she took his hard dick into her hands and slowly licked around his tip. She took him into her mouth and sucked his head while tickling his balls. His head fell back and he bit his lips.

"Fuck ma." He hissed and Troi grinned. Sonny's eyes were rolling to the back of his head. In his twenty-one of years of living he never had head like this. Troi was taking his soul and he was giving it to her willingly, she could have anything she wanted if it was up to him.

The vibrations from her hums everytime he hit the back of her throat brought him near climax. *Yeah, I got this nigga right where I want him. I know he never had head like this before. Troi for the win.* She thought to herself as she watched Sonny clench his eyes shut. Troi finally released him from her mouth and blew on his tip. It was like the kiss of death, the simple gesture caused Sonny to erupt like a volcano. Troi stood to her feet and Sonny looked at her with wide eyes. She'd done some shit to him that he'd never experienced.

"Hell nah, bring yo ass on." Sonny washed himself and Troi then carried her to the bedroom and threw her on his bed. Troi had outdone herself and although he wasn't a pro in head he'd mastered slanging dick. Sonny folded Troi's legs up, turning her to a human pretzel as he plunged his dick inside her. Sonny knew his way around pussy once he was inside. As he found her g-spot and made sure to tap it every time. As he went deeper and deeper he drove Troi wild. Tears filled in the brim of her eye from the depth in which his dick touched.

"Fuck Sonny. Wait-a-min pleaseeeee. Daddy, right there don't stop." Troi wanted Sonny to take her to heaven and that's exactly where he was taking her.

"Nah, you think you about to take my soul and I don't take yours. Huh, that's what you thought." He growled on her ear as he used his thumb to start playing with her clit. The feeling was so magical, tears fell from her eyes. She didn't want him to stop. The pleasure was the best she'd ever felt. Troi couldn't do anything but lay there and let him take her soul. She now knew why women allowed Sonny to act a fool and still gave him ass. It was because he knew how to work every part of a woman's body. His arrogance was overshadowed by his bedroom game. They both felt the nearing climax and Troi allowed him to stay in her nest.

Slowly pulling out of Troi, Sonny was about to put her on all fours but Troi gained her strength and pushed Sonny onto his back. She squatted over him, sitting on his dick backwards. Troi rode Sonny like she was on a mechanical bull. She grinded on him slowly giving him a nice view of her ass and his dick as she bounced. Sonny sat on his elbows and slapped his hand across her soft ass. It lightly jiggled making him want to bite it.

"Cum with me daddy." That was all he heard before he exploded for a second time. Troi came onto him and spun on his dick facing him in the process. She leaned over to him kissing him on the lips then laid her head onto his chest.

As she caught her breath she looked up at Sonny and he was sleeping like a baby. Troi smirked and put on her clothes. The sun was beginning to rise and it was time for her to get going. She and Sonny had both indulged in what they both wanted and it was time to make an exit. She knew of Sonny and his Sonny ways and Troi wasn't trying to get caught up in it.

Chapter 11

"I still can't believe you let him go, you know Jose is fucking dead Selena. What the fuck was going through your mind." Alejandro was furious, if he would have killed Llanzo when he had the chance Genie wouldn't have been missing. It had been twelve hours since Genie had been snatched up and Alejandro was blaming his sister for everything. His stomach churned at the thought of where she was and what they were doing with her. Genie was his only daughter and after hours of scouring the streets and looking for her they had come up with nothing.

"No, No. Don't you dare go blaming that on me. She's my niece too. My son is gone and never coming back. You would have done the same thing to get Genie back. If one of those pendejo's walked they ass in here giving you hope on her being alive you would take it! You didn't know how I felt. But now you know how I feel." By now tears was falling from Selena eyes. How dare he blame her for Genie being missing. Selena was furious and the pain in her eyes was evidence that she was overwhelmed. Their family was taking multiple losses and the blame game was like throwing gasoline onto the wildfire.

"I'm not blaming you, I just want my daughter back." Sitting behind his desk Alejandro put his hands behind his head and sighed deeply. "They want five million dollars for proof! They are trying to milk me fucking dry." Alejandro barked already knowing what Llanzo was attempting. Five million for proof of life was bullshit. That wasn't how shit usually went down and Alejandro was unsure if he wanted to give in. "Do I want to go in guns blazing or just pay this fuckers the five mill." He asked himself out loud. Alejandro was in deep thoughts, trying to figure out his next move. They'd outsmarted him for the first time and Alejandro wanted to flip the script.

"Just pay the man, stop trying to always have one up on the Vados. Can we just end the war already. We've already lost Jose. We can't lose Genesis too." Selena placed her back against the wall feeling defeated. The bloodshed was paying a toll on her mentally and emotionally. The tears began flooding her face causing her body to begin shaking as she cried. With all the shit that's been going on with the two family, she wouldn't be surprised if her niece was dead.

Lifting her head up she frowned at her brother, and stood up wiping her face. "You know what, Alejandro. You are going to pay him to get Genie back." Selena's face was red eyes were puffy and nose was sore. "Let's not forget. You're the reason this bullshit war started in the first place!"

"Don't you dare bring that up, that's in the past and our kids have nothing to do with it. They don't know shit about that!" Alejandro defended weakly knowing Selena was right. The DeLeon's and Vado's beef went back twenty years and the reminder of him being the cause of it all made his head spin. Twenty years had been such a long time ago and he couldn't believe he was just now receiving his karma.

"Alejandro wi have tuh stop tis, DaJuan isn't dumb him is going to find out." Amoi sat up in the bed covering her body. Her conscience was eating at her like it did everytime they were together. There was a thin line between fear and her conscience. Alejandro moved the cover and admired Amoi's body as he closed the space between them. It was something about a Jamacian lover that drove him crazy. Just the thought of the way Amoi rode him the night before had his dick standing up at attention.

"You let me worry about DaJuan, all you have to do is keep sitting pretty and collecting both of our money." He consoled her as he showered her with kisses all over her neck. Alejandro was ready to have another round with Amoi. Every time he seen her he wanted to overdose on that pussy. He slowly laid her back on the bed, and climbed on top of her.

"Is that all mih worth? Sitting pretty?" Wrapping her hands around Alejandro's neck, Amoi kissed his soft lips, sticking her tongue down his throat.

"You're worth that and so much more, if I could have it my way you'll be my wife."

"Mih love mih husband. When mih become a widow then maybe. Right now DaJuan and mih share kids. If I try to leave him he will kill me and my kids need me. He can't raise dem." Amoi pushed him off of her and stood up off the bed. "Yuh cannot fall in luv wit mih Alejandro. Mih husband is yuh business partner." Turning around Amoi bent down to get her clothes so she could shower and go to her husband.

Alejandro stood behind her and slid his dick inside Amoi's love box catching her by surprise making her forget all about DaJuan.

"Alejandro." Amoi moaned as she touched her toes while he filled the depths of her soul.

"Alejandro…Alejandro…Alejandro!" Selena calling him brought him back. "Let me guess you was thinking about the bitch who caused all this drama huh? You're never gonna learn."

Turning to leave out the door Selena turned to Alejandro one last time. "Dales el dinero y encuentra a mi maldita sobrina." (Give them the money and get my niece) Walking out she bumped right into her nephew Gunz.

"What the fuck happened!?" He yelled enraged, ready to find his sister.

"Ask your stupid ass papa!" Selena hurried up the stairs into the guest room to continue grieving her son. Her loss was heavy now that Genie had now been snatched up. She barely had faith. But still in the back of her mind, hope lived in her. And Selena was hoping her dumb ass brother made the right decision.

***

Sunlight crept through the blinds, causing Sonny to wake up. He hadn't remembered falling asleep. As he slowly opened his eyes, his naked frame on his silk sheets caused him to recollect his memory. *Troi put that NyQuil pussy on me.* He let out a boyish grin while sitting up in the bed.

Sonny looked around the room and although he remembered Troi being in bed with him there was no trace of her. He only had a wet dick to show for it and Sonny's ego was instantly bruised. Troi had flipped the roles. *She got me fucked up.*

Sonny was feeling played, he walked into the master bathroom getting in the shower washing Troi's scent off of him. For the first time ever he was dreading this part. Troi had put some shit down on him and put him to sleep. *Bitch ain't even leave a note, no money, nothing.* Sonny sucked his teeth and hurriedly made it out the shower. The longer he thought about Troi ditching him the madder he became. He had never thought he'd be on the other end of the stick and hated every minute of it. Sonny had prided himself on fucking bitches and leaving before they opened their eyes but Troi had beat him to it.

He brushed his teeth and headed into his closet ready to check Troi. He hadn't thought about what he would say just yet, but he had time to figure it out before he got there. Sonny settled on a crisp fitted white tank top that revealed his tatted skin, blue and black fatigue Bathing Ape shorts with a wide frown across his jewel and a pair of black retro 9s. He stared in the mirror and the look of his dreads frizzed up caused him to grill himself in the mirror. *Bitch made me eat that voodoo pussy and fucked my hair up.* The more Sonny thought to himself about Troi the more angrier he became.

Sonny looked for the keys to his Benz and realized that he'd left it at The Underground. He never left his car, if anyone was leaving a car it had to be a bitch. Sonny replaying the events of last night made him realize how much he switched up his cadence for Troi. He'd done it so easily for her that it scared him. *That bitch is the devil.* Sonny snatched up the keys to his BMW and headed into his garage, thankful that he wasn't a bum ass nigga with only one car.

Have mercy on me, have mercy on my soul

Don't let my heart turn cold

Pop Smoke blared through Sonny's speakers as he drove to Troi's house like a bat that made it out of hell. He still hadn't wrapped his head around what he would be saying to her, Sonny just had to see her. Troi had beat him at his own game and he needed to check her, at least that's what he told himself. Because everytime he thought of her his dick jumped. The way she's put it on him had put him to sleep like a baby. A gift and a curse all in one. Sonny's phone rang but he decided against answering it. When he saw it was Troi he sucked his teeth.

"Don't call a nigga now. Say what you gotta say when you see me," Sonny mumbled to himself as he pulled up to Troi's home. Before he could fully park his car Troi walked out of her home looking like an Instagram model. Her dreads were put up in a bun high on her head, a tye dye blue long sleeve dress that stopped way before her knee hugged her every curve, and silver gladiator heels blessed her feet. Sonny's face frowned up as he watched her get into her car. Everything in him wanted to get out of the car but he decided against it.

Instead he followed her fifteen minutes from her home until they were in front of a restaurant. *She better be*

Sonny couldn't even process the thought that he was thinking when he saw Troi walk over to a slim cream colored man who stood at about six feet, with a slight salt and pepper beard and a fade. He was clean, slacks and a button down. The kind of nigga that looked like a fucking square. When Sonny watched the man's hand roam over Troi's ass he almost lost it. He quickly jumped out of his car and headed over to the pair.

"Yo Troi, what type of shit you on?" He called out as he walked up on them.

Troi's eyes widened in surprise as Sonny stood in front of her grilling her like he wanted to wring her neck.

"Yo who is this kid?" The guy grilled Sonny back as a smirk tugged his lips. Troi felt like evaporating into thin air. A showdown between her boyfriend and a one night stand couldn't be pretty. Their animosity alone had wondering eyes peering over at them.

"Nigga who the fuck is you?" Sonny barked at him. His anger was getting the very best of him. Another man trying to son him made him ready to put a hot one in him and Troi could see the fire between his eyes.

"Sonny let's talk," Troi tried reaching for his arm to deescalate the situation but it was too late. Sonny was on go.

"Nah fuck that, let's talk about why you ain't got no fucking panties on. You was about to go fuck this nigga too? What type of slide shit you on?"

"Sonny stop!" Troi yelled, the embarrassment he was causing her didn't go unnoticed. Sonny was seeing red and although everything he was saying was to Troi he was looking directly at her boyfriend waiting for him to jump so he could have a reason to blow his ass away to neverland. A nigga like this couldn't handle a bitch like Troi. Nothing about her screamed that she liked a weak ass nigga like the one in front of Sonny.

"Too? You fucked this lil ass boy?" Her boyfriend chuckled as he gave her a disapproving look. His words triggered Sonny for a second time and before he could answer Sonny closed the space between them as his gun pressed firmly onto the man's rib.

"Whose a lil nigga?" He growled, the dude's hand went up in defeat but it was too late. Sonny's finger was a few seconds off the trigger and he was ready to silence ole boy in broad daylight. Hotheaded, not giving a fuck who was around them. If he was going to jail his brother's would see to it that he came home. If Troi's nigga wanted smoke than Sonny was bringing a cannon.

"Carson!" Troi yelled at him placing her hand under his chin and turning his face towards her. "Put it the fuck away," she demanded frantically. Her heart was beating like African drums and she couldn't think straight. Everything was happening too fast. Sonny was set off so easily and she was the only one that could get him calm. He was like the tazmanian devil and Troi was his music. The only person that could calm him down and be his voice of reasoning. Sonny heard the fear in her voice and that brought him back to reality. He tucked his gun in his waistband and grabbed Troi closer to him letting his hand roam over her ass before placing his lips on hers.

"She saved you nigga. And you not getting your bitch back. Tell your niggas how a lil nigga took your bitch." Sonny taunted as he slapped her ass. Troi's entire body was heated. Between the embarrassment, and the gangster Sonny had displayed, he had turned her on a little. She instantly regretted not wearing panties. Sonny stared at her with a boyish grin and licked her lips. "You gon get these niggas fucked up everytime you walk out the crib without drawers. Only time you supposed to freeball is when you in my house so I can have easy access to the pussy." Sonny scolded as he led her back to his car, making Troi have to clench her legs together or her juices was going to be rolling down her legs.

"My car,"

"Nobody want that Honda, I'll buy you a new one. Just let me taste that voodoo pussy again." He joked as he let her into his car before driving off.

Chapter 12

Knock knock

Imani's eyebrows raised as she wondered who was at her door. Nobody was allowed to just show up announced, and Imani had already made up her mind that she wouldn't open the door. She was hoping the person on the other end would leave. *Motherfucking Jehovas Witness persistent as fuck.*

Imani thought as the knock began again, this time more frantically. She rolled her eyes as she walked over to the door to see who it was.

A disoriented Nitro stood at the other end of her door as she looked through the peephole and Imani's eyebrows instantly furrowed together. She swung her door open and rolled her eyes even harder as he stood in the doorway with a toy poodle in his hand that wore a Diamond encrusted *I* necklace. Imani's eyes melted as she quickly grabbed the pup from his hand.

"Say what's up to my nigga Icy" Imani's happy face slowly began melting down as she realized what Nitro was doing.

"Thank you for the dog, but you can leave," Imani folded her arms. Nitro was taken aback by her sudden change in attitude. He'd seen that he'd won her over and just that quick she remembered how he played her.

"Mani stop being like that. A nigga need you right now." Nitro entered her home, closing the door behind him.

Every part of Imani wanted to turn him away but she couldn't. She'd heard about the loss his family had taken. Everyone had heard and everyday she'd wondered how Nitro was holding up but her pride wouldn't allow her to call him to check up on him. And now that he'd shown up, it was hard for Imani to let her insecurities go. They seemed so minor at a time where he was experiencing unexplainable pain.

She slowly slid the Diamond necklace off Icy and placed her onto the floor. The small brown pup instantly took off ready to take advantage of her new home.

"Did you bring piss pads? I don't want him pissing all over my house."

Nitro gave Imani a small smirk from behind. "Nah, you gon have to give me a list for all the shit I need. That lil nigga definitely peed twice in my car before I got here."

Imani plopped onto the couch pulling the cover to her neck as she pressed play on her movie. "Yo how many times you gonna watch this shit?" He sat beside her and pulled her into his lap.

"Shrek is a classic. You can't get tired of it. Plus it's Sunday. You knew what time it was. Or maybe you forgot." Imani rolled her eyes and wiggled out his grasp. Nitro was everything to her. Him playing her the way he did hurt her to the core. Not only was her ego bruised but Imani's heart was broken.

"I knew that shit was coming one way or another. What a nigga gotta do to make you forget about that?"

"Forget you walking off with another bitch that you allowed to be disrespectful?" The more Imani talked about it the more anger consumed her. Because she'd replayed the moment in her mind a million times and the outcome had never sat right in her soul.

"I said I'm sorry ma. That shit was fucked up and I shouldn't have tried to play you like that." He pulled her back into him this time kissing her on her neck while holding her in a grasp where she couldn't move.

"Nah you really played me. And I don't think you can take the kind of hurt that imma give your ass back."

Nitro instantly let go of her. The thought of Imani being on the other end of the betrayal stick burned him up inside.

"Yea Aight, don't get fucked up out here trying to be cute Mani,"

POP

Her fist connected with Nitro's jaw. "You don't get to make threats to nobody. You violated me when you walked away with the next bitch in tow. You thought you was about to come over with that cute ass dog and get some pussy but obviously you got the wrong bitch." Imani's rant caused her to pause her movie. She was on go and she needed to blow the steam off her chest. She'd waited for the day he showed his face at her door and although it had taken a few weeks seeing him ignited her rage again.

"Keep your fucking hands to yourself." Nitro warned. He and Imani both stared at one another like they were ready for a showdown. Imani's phone began ringing and she quickly sent it to voicemail.

"You're right. I'll keep my hands and this fire ass pussy to myself. The next nigga gon luck up."

"The next nigga gon be in a ditch and that's word to Chas."
Imani's phone began ringing again and instantly Nitro's annoyance
had heightened. The caller on the other line was persistent.
He picked up her phone and Imani tried snatching it back. But she
was too late. The phone was already in Nitro's ear.

"Gimme back my fucking phone." She tried reaching over
him but Nitro held her back with one hand and kept the phone to his
ear.

"This ain't Mani nigga. You blowing up my bitch phone like
you pay the bill. Delete her number or imma find you and"

Before he could finish his sentence Imani quickly grabbed
the phone hanging it up. "Oh you panicking, that's what ya sneaky
ass doing?"

"Fuck you Denetro, you left me for another bitch!"

"Scream that shit from a mountain all you want. I said I was
fucking sorry. You giving your number out to niggas? Change your
shit, cause word to everything imma start dropping your niggas. So
save yourself the tears." Nitro stood from his seat and walked
towards the door but headed back towards Imani. He gave her a peck
on her lips and ran his finger over them.

"Imma see you later" he promised as he walked out her apartment. He had to tighten up. Genie had him fucked up and her betrayal was worse than any other woman's betrayal he'd experienced. Imani had never, would never plot on him and he was realizing he fucked up. She was his ride or die. Nitro was good on playing women close at this point in his life. It never worked out and after answering Imani's phone it was clear she was playing hard ball.

***

Really gonna miss you, its really gonna be different without you time is gonna be hard and slow, for the rest of my life gonna be thinking about you yes I am, time came when you had to go

Cher sat on her bed in her white off shoulder dress, listening to Smokie Robinson *Really Gonna Miss You*. Black wasn't allowed at Chasity 's funeral. She wanted her daughter's funeral to be peaceful, not gloomy. Her life was gloomy enough and her daughter not having a life any longer added to it.

Getting off the bed she walked into her walk-in closet and took a seat at her vanity. The closet was so spacious it was like another bedroom inside of her bedroom. Cher looked at herself in the mirror and couldn't help the fresh pool of tears that filled them. She placed her head in her hand and let out a sob. Her tears were because Chasity 's life was taken so young and she would never get to experience anything more. She wouldn't get to have her first boyfriend, she wouldn't get to go to any homecoming nor prom, no husband and children, her baby girl wouldn't have anything. She would never go to Summer Jam at sixteen. All the work and years Cher put into raising Chas felt like nothing anymore. Like it didn't matter.

"Chasity baby, mama is so sorry." Grabbing a wet cloth she wiped her face and started to do her makeup. For Chas she was beating her face, as she would say. Fifteen minutes later Cher's light make up was done. She couldn't do too much without tears rushing her face.

"Yuh ready to go? I have a surprise for yuh and di limo outside." Rich entered her closet looking fine as ever. His red and white Gucci's shirt and all-white Gucci slacks with the matching loafers made him look crisp. His black skin glistened and his dreads were pulled into a ponytail as shades covered his eyes.

"Yeah I guess so." She didn't have shit to say to Rich. She was only fucking with him for her kids sake. Walking out in front of him she got her sons and walked out the front door.

Once they were inside the Limo the atmosphere was dull and gloomy. Like they just entered a tunnel of depression.

She was wondering what was taking Rich so long to get into the limo and when the door opened her best friend Wynter climbed inside.

"Wynni! Oh my God. How are you, why are you, how are you here right now." Cher's shock was evident. It was a relief. Wynni brought a sense of sunlight everywhere she went. She pulled Cher into her and Cher cried into her neck. Wynni's presence was needed. Her best friend was the only person she could express her grief to.

"You know I wouldn't miss my baby funeral." It was then that Cher looked in Wynni's eyes and saw the pain behind them. Wynter was there for it all. Every pregnancy, and every labor and delivery visit, she'd made it. And it was obvious her showing up didn't stop there because here she was at Chas's funeral. They held onto one another the entire way to the church. Cher was grateful for her presence. She'd needed her.

As they pulled up to the church where Chasity's funeral was being held, Cher smiled thinking about how everyone came to send her baby off. Estranged family members, old friends, Chasity's classmates. Everyone had come to show their respect.

Nitro, Sonny and Kill greeted them the minute they stood in front of the church. They all matched their brother's fly with Gucci sunglasses on. They formed a circle around Cher and an overwhelming urge took over her. *Why didn't they protect my baby like this?* Cher cried into Sonny's chest because he was the closest to her and the only one who looked like he was hanging on by a thread. His eyes were just as puffy as hers and he didn't try to conceal it. Each brother mourned in their own way and although her loss was a heavy one she felt for them as well. They might have got on her nerves, but this moment mattered the most to her. They was here when she needed them the most.

"Mommy do we get to see sissy now." Legend was holding on to his daddy leg. How were they supposed to explain to their five year old son that his sister wasn't coming back. His best friend of all friends and his protector was dead. He didn't know what any of it meant, all he knew was that something wasn't right. Where was his sister?

"What's up Gee." Kill picked his nephew up and hugged him.

"Where's sissy Uncle K." Legend lifted the sunglasses off his Kill's eyes and his eyes were bloodshot. He hadn't gotten any sleep since Chasity was killed. The pain in his eyes broke Cher even more. Rich couldn't even look at his son, he was grateful for his brother stepping in.

"Cher can I talk to you before we walk in the church." Rich put his arms around his wife's waist, practically begging her to talk to him. Nodding her head she stepped away with her husband behind her. Once they were far enough where no one could hear, they started at each other for a second. "I know I'm on yo shit list and I know you don't want shit to do with me but Ma can we at least act like we get along. I need you by my side today and I know you need me by your side."

As much as Cher didn't want to, she knew Rich was right. She needed her husband. She needed him so bad that it made her heart hurt.

"You're right, let's do this for Chasity ." Stepping to Rich she reached up and hugged him around his neck. This was the closest she'd been to her husband in the last week. Walking hand and hand they stood in front of the church with the brothers behind them. All with shades on, so people couldn't see them broken. They were Vados, the strongest family in Georgia. Weaknesses were not a part of them. Walking into the church Rich and Cher stopped before making it to the casket.

Chasity was beautiful. Her yellow dress with diamonds on it, matched her skin tone perfectly. The smile on her face let everyone know she was at peace. Her pink casket was the topping on the cake. The yellow tulips were her favorite and they were all around her casket and around the church. Rich spared no expense when it came to his daughter. Dropping ten bands on a casket was nothing but painful because shit wasn't supposed to go like that. He would give her anything he just wished she were still there.

"Come on ma. We have to do this." Rich guided his wife to his daughter casket and that was all it took for her to break down. Leaning on the casket Cher cried and cried.

"Chasity please come back home to me. Mommy baby please don't do this to me. I'll do anything, you can get blowouts and wear makeup. You can do whatever you want but please come back to me." Wynter stood behind the couple for support. Although she wasn't, Rich's biggest fan right now but now wasn't the time to be petty. There wasn't a dry eye in the room, Cher had everyone in tears, even the brothers had tears leaking from their chins.

"I love you baby girl. You'll always be daddy's little girl." Rich leaned in and kissed her on the cheek. As much as he wanted to break he couldn't because he had to be strong for his wife. His family had bought her this pain and he wished he could reverse it.

Walking up to the casket Kill held Legend in his hands. "Wake up sissy." Legend was trying to get out his uncle's hands to get to his sissy. He didn't understand why Chas wasn't talking back.

"Sissy can't wake up nephew. But listen to me you're sister is always in your heart. Remember this for me okay. Give sissy a kiss." Leaning in Kill and Legend both kissed Chasity before taking their seat next to Cher and Rich.

Sonny made it to the casket and broke. Not one to show emotions, he was hurt and this was something that wasn't sitting well with him. Nitro put his arms around his baby brother and cried with him. This was by far the hardest thing they ever had to do. Saying goodbye to their parents who'd experienced life hadn't hit them this hard. Chas was a baby. Caught a disrespectful stray bullet. They never wanted to say goodbye to her, she was supposed to bury them not the other way around.

"I got him." Sonny heard her voice and when the smell of her Gucci Bloom Eau de Parfum invaded his nose, he looked up and Troi was standing there. She'd become his shorty so easily. Everything about her was easy. Troi was gentle because she'd heard about Sonny the beast. She liked the Sonny she brought out more though and so did he. Troi's presence made him feel better. He wrapped his arms around her waist and cried on her chest. His guard was all the way down. He'd already been weak because of his loss but Troi disarmed him. She didn't see him as being weak, but Sonny felt it. Troi saw a broken uncle ready for revenge. After the family paid their respects to Chasity, the rest of the church viewed her body and gave their condolences.

The entire funeral was a big blur for Cher and Rich, they didn't hear anything the pastor said. Their eyes were stuck on the casket that their oldest baby was laying lifeless in. Both trying to figure out where life would take them. What were they going to do without her? Nothing, their life wasn't nothing without her. She'd made them parents.

After the funeral everyone followed the horse and carriage to Chasity 's final resting spot. Cher couldn't handle it so she and Wynter stayed and watched from the limo. She couldn't see her daughter be put into the ground.

The four brothers stood around Chasity's gravesite putting flowers on it before they lowered her into the ground. Everyone left after the pastor said his last prayer. The scene was heartbreaking as they all gathered around Rich. They'd lost a niece but he lost a daughter. He lost his only daughter and nothing could top that pain. Falling to his knees Rich cried as they lowered his daughter in the ground. Kill, Sonny, and Nitro stood behind their brother with silent tears falling.

"My baby man, my fucking baby is gone." Hopping up Rich tried to stop them from lowering her in the ground but his brothers held him back. He fought and fought, they couldn't lower her. Not without him. If they were burying her, they were burying him.

"Bro, let them do their job." Kill grabbed a hold of his brother and bearhugged him. Rich was too strong right now though, no one could keep him from Chasity. He wasn't ready to let go.

"Get the fuck off me Akiel. Don't let them bury her. She needs me." Rich cried. Seeing the scene from afar, Cher got out of the limo and rushed to her husband with Wynni right behind her. Cher slipped her heels off her feet and walked barefoot in the grass. She kneeled beside him and placed her hand onto Rich's back and he knew it was her without turning around. Cher pulled him into her. She felt his pain. She'd never seen Rich this way.

"Cher don't let them bury our baby." Rich brought Cher down with him. By this time they were putting the dirt on top of the casket. Rich laid his head in Cher lap and cried as Kill, Sonny, Nitro and Wynni watched them with their own tears falling. Chasity was gone and there wasn't nothing they could do about it.

Chapter 13

"Has someone taken your order?" Kill asked a couple at the table. Today he was working at Footprints. He'd been taking over since Rich and Cher needed time off. They were mourning in a way that just required them to be together so Kill stepped up. He handled the family's street business and legal business. He worked his grief off. Kill didn't indulge in his emotions as much as his brothers. Because all his life he saw how emotions were the downfall of so many men. So he tucked his, not ready to die yet. Kill hadn't truly lived yet. He had worked hard, and hustled harder. All for a great cause, he had plans to settle down and maybe have kids one day. The day didn't have an expiration date on it. The day existed only because the thought existed. Kill hadn't added much to the thought. Because for now he was a worker. He was adding to the solid foundation that his family had put down. Paying his dues, making sure their legacy lived for more years to come. Kill hurried into the kitchen where everyone looked like they were putting in over time.

"I need the plates for table two," Kill ordered. Today was one of their busiest days in the year. Atlanta Carribean Carnival, had everyone and their mother outside. Women in their different colorful costumes filled their restaurant. Feathers, body paint, and gems all over the melanated women brought joy to Kill. One thing he loved was laying his eyes on beautiful women.

"You look like you need help," Kaylin's voice came from behind him as she placed an apron over her head.

"You always pick the best time to pop in on a nigga." Kill winked.

"My bestie senses be tingling telling me you need my help."

"Nah nigga, your nosey senses be ringing and now your nosey ass ain't got no choice but to help." Kill passed her a tray of food. He watched as Kaylin giggled as she waltzed away. He already knew Kaylin was coming for. They'd been friends long enough and she was deadass about the bestie senses. Somehow Kaylin always knew when Kill was off even when he didn't show it. She quickly reentered the kitchen with dishes on her tray.

"Next year, I want a carnival costume. That's how you can pay me for this shift I'm working."

"You came to keep a nigga company?" Kill asked with a smirked ready to jump into what was so heavily on Kaylin's mind.

She was thirsty to jump right into it and his stalling was driving her crazy, but it didn't matter.

"I came to make sure you ain't been keeping no bad company." Kills brow's arched together as he grabbed Kaylin's hand and let her into the back of the kitchen.

"You want to talk about it, let's go. Cause that was a low blow." Kaylin didn't have to say much. The little she said had been heard loud and clear.

"Was it a low blow? I saw the way you left the hotel. I saw how you were overprotective at the funeral. Not only did I see it but I felt it. I felt you pull away. You never fucking pull away. So what was that about? And you working here now?"

Kill ran his hand alongside his jaw before closing in the space between him and Kaylin. All of her assumptions were wrong and he needed her to never put it back in the universe again. "Nah what you saw was me handling family business. Cause that shit always come first. So if I pulled, it was just my priority." Kill grilled before walking away. His words pissed Kaylin off.

"So that bitch is a priority?" Kaylin asked as she snagged her neck. She wanted Kill to choose his next words carefully because she was seconds from showing her black ass in there.

"Akiel," Cher's confused voice made the hairs on the back of his neck stand up. Like he'd been caught doing something he wasn't supposed to be doing. Kaylin felt the pull again and rolled her eyes at Cher. She hadn't been mistaken and Kill almost had her fooled. That first name basis shit was only for bitches you would pull a trigger for. Kaylin knew it because once upon a time she was the only one who called him by his first name. Kill hadn't corrected Cher like he'd done plenty of hoes in different cities.

"Kill, Mi need yuh tuh cum wid mi." Rich waved him over as he entered the kitchen.

Saved by the bell. Kill was out of the hot seat. He rushed over to Rich not asking any questions. He just could feel the showdown waiting to happen. And he wasn't with it.

"What are you doing back here?" Cher gave Kaylin the attitude right back to her. They were having a pissing match. Two women who had love for the same man. One feeling more superior than the other.

"Akiel brought me here,"

"Well you need to get out. I'll talk to him about having his bitches in here." Cher grilled getting disrespectful and Kaylin caught it. She scoffed and rolled her eyes as she walked away.

"Bitch please, like you ain't been auditioning for the part." Kaylin stormed off leaving Cher to pick her jaw up off the floor.

You got the right one bitch. Kaylin thought as she walked out of the kitchen. She hadn't heard a reply back from Cher. So she knew she hit it out of the ballpark. It wasn't all in her head. Kill and Cher's connection was real and to the naked eye you couldn't really tell. Only Kaylin could feel it because she loved Akiel with her entire heart and she could feel the frequency in their connection when Cher was around.

***

"Yuh ready tuh get this shit ova wid dis bitch. I'm ready to put a bullet in her." Rich and Kill walked into the room where Genie was being held. She looked up, saw them and mugged them hard. She hated that she had got caught slipping by them. Her slipping had cost her family five million dollars. In the game of war, the Vado family was finally winning.

"Fuck you Punta." She spat on the ground by Rich feet. Spitting was disrespectful and the DeLeon's didn't have any more passes on being disrespectful. He pulled his gun out placing it under her chin ready to end her.

"Yuh hungry." Kill stepped in between them placing his hand over his brothers. He sympathized with him. Rich's need for revenge poured from his pores.

Rich took a step back knowing that Genie would be dead fucking with him so he had to keep his distance. Kill untied her hands and passed her the Mexican food.

Genie held the plate and looked over it and launched it as far as it would go. She would never trust them. If she was gonna die she wouldn't voluntarily do it. She tried using the little bit of strength she did have to try and untie her feet. Her body was bruised and battered and even the simplest task took so much work.

"Kill fuck her, let's make tis video so wi can go." Rich pulled out out his burner phone and started recording, he didnt give a fuck how she looked.

"Yuh have someting tuh say to yuh family?" Rich taunted her. This would be the last they heard from her so Genie had to make it good. Her life was on a countdown and everyone knew it.

"I'm not saying shit." Genie grilled him. She was like an angry pitbull. Even with her lack of energy.

"Yuh don't have tuh say shit." Taking the phone from Rich, Kill turned the camera toward his big brother. "Listen tuh mih, if yuh want tis bitch back you'll have the rest of mih money transferred tuh dat account. After Mih get the fifteen million, mih will tell yuh where yuh can pick this bitch up from."

"No, No! Papi, don't send them anything. Voy a averiguar a papa! No envies nada a estas perras! Cuando salgamons por ellos, se dirigen! DeLeon's hasta el fondo de mi! (I'm going to find away out daddy. Don't send these bitches nothing. When I'm out we coming for they heads. DeLeons until the death of me). Kill cut the video off as she spoke so quickly they couldn't even try to attempt to interpret what she was saying. All the energy she didn't have seemed to come back like the video was a shot of espresso.

Rich had no clue what she said but he was furious. His body was hot. Kill turned the video back on ready to re-record but Rich had enough.

"Bitch wat di fuck yuh just say. Speak english." Grabbing Genie by her throat, Rich slouched down to her level to be face to face with her. Genie just smiled at him, knowing that she was getting under his skin. She wouldn't say a word. They were demanding shit and she would give them hell. There was no way she would let these niggas body her. She was a bitch who didn't back down and wasn't scared of anything. She was a nigga worst nightmare and Rich knew Genie would go toe to toe with him. "I'm going tuh make sure mih have fun wit yuh before we send yuh back. Cut it off Kill." Rich wanted to make sure Kill caught his last sentence before telling him to send that video to Alejandro.

"I'll have fun with yo brothers, especially the one you call Nitro. Next time send him to come see me." The only thing she needed for them to do was send Nitro to check on her instead of this crazy muthafucka Rich. As crazy as Rich was, Kill's silence and poise feared her most. Motherfuckers barked loud but their bite was soft. It was the ones who didn't bark at all that would tear shit up.

She could see Kill letting Rich get his steam off. But still, Rich didn't faze her. Her daddy always told her, never underestimate the quiet ones. She was more scared of Kill than she was Rich.

"You gone eat?" Kill honestly didn't want to kill this woman let alone let Rich torture her. He would take from her because Genie's family had taken from him. He would scar Genie for life. All of Rich's thoughts that Genie occupied came with hatred.

Kill could see Genie trying to keep up and stay alive. He could admit. The bitch didn't break. But he felt bad for her. Genie could easily be swapped out with Kaylin or Cher. The DeLeons had already touched Chas and although they had Genie the DeLeon's were just as good at this game.

Kill was ready to get it over with, he still stuck to the rules. Women and children to be untouched. Even though Chasity was caught in the crossfire, he knew that bullet was meant for one of them. He would have gladly taken it. .

"No, I'm not hungry just get yo rapey ass brother away from me." Genie needed to be alone to think of her plan to get out. She was getting weaker by the second and Rich's plans for her made her stomach turn.

"We out Rich." Kill tapped his brother on the shoulder. He walked over to Genie and began tying her arms back up. If he didn't get Rich out of there the look in his eyes told him he was ready to risk it all. Say fuck the money and kill Genie. Twenty million dollars wasn't shit compared to Chasity life.

He was into the law of retaliation. He wanted a life for a life and if it had to be Genie then so fucking be it. They say a woman scorned wasn't nothing to play with but they never saw a father scorned. Rich was out for blood and as soon as he got Genie alone, the bitch was going to meet Chasity .

Rich doubled back and looked at her before he walked out the door with Kill. Her days were numbered, Rich was already counting down.

Chapter 14

The light from the door opening woke Genie up. A week of starvation was taking a toll on her. She was feeling borderline crazy. Like she was lingering between life and death. Genesis was losing hope. Maybe she would die here. For her family she would. She had that DeLeon blood in her. Her family's empire had been built a little over twenty years ago. They stood for something, so they didn't fall for anything. Genie finally looked up, and when her eyes adjusted to the light and saw Nitro her heart weakened. *How the fuck did I fall for the fucking enemy.* She looked behind him at the door wondering if he'd come alone. Nitro closed the door and locked it.

"What the fuck are you doing here Nitro?" Genie stood her ground but she was happy her plan was finally about to come true. She was getting the fuck out of there today.

"You was plotting on me and my fucking brothers this whole time?" Nitro pulled up a chair and sat in front of Genie. The smell that came from her burned his nose. A mixture of urine, shit, and blood. He almost felt bad for her. They finally had alone time, and this was the best time to be here. Six o'clock in the morning on a

Sunday. Hopefully God was in the building because the two had bones to pick.

"If I knew you killed my cousin, I wouldn't have ever fucked with you. I would have left you where the fuck you were at." Genie mustered up all her strength to talk. She wasn't intimidated and although she didn't have much strength, Nitro hadn't known her to be anything but strong.

"Yes you would have. If I would've killed your daddy, you still would've given me the pussy." Nitro said knowingly. He could see Genie trying to get under his skin but it wasn't happening he'd already got into hers and he could do it again. Nitro was ready to call her bluff. But first he had to feed her. Genie was unkept. Looked so much different from the women he met at the club. His brothers had done a number on her and he could tell if she didn't eat she would probably not make it another day. He opened the bag of food he'd brought with him and opened it up. He took a scoop first putting it in his mouth allowing her to watch him consume the food first.

"See, a nigga ain't out to get you." He told her as he scooped up another spoon and put it to her lips. He was feeding her like a baby, to give her some strength and nourish her. Genie wanted to hesitate but she didn't. She was starving and the plan she'd put in place she would need it.

In less than five minutes the large order of curry chicken, potatoes and roti was completed and Genie finally looked like he'd given her a little life.

"You want to take a shower and get cleaned up a little." Looking back Nitro made sure he locked the door cause he couldn't trust her. As far as he knew he'd fell into Genie's plan easily the first time and he wasn't trying to a second time.

"That's the least you can do." He untied her hand and grabbed her by the arm guiding her to the small bathroom.

This must be what heaven feels like. The hot water cascaded down Genie's skin making her finally feel relief. She hadn't showered in so long her stench made her sick. The water was at the highest temperature she could stand it, and she made sure not to let it hit her gunshot wounds directly. The doctor Rich had brought to see her did the fucking miminal. The water ran over her hair opening her pores. Genie scrubbed her scalp until it started to hurt and she scrubbed her body until it was raw. She wanted all the dirt gone.

.

Nitro stood by the door watching her clean herself. His dick was standing at attention wanting to be freed from his pants. The head in between his legs had a mind of its own.

Once Genie stepped out of the shower she and Nitro locked eyes again. The fire in both of their eyes told a story only they knew. Hatred and love was equal in that moment. Genie was in love with this bad boy that hated her family, but her family came first. Nitro didn't care though. He stepped towards Genie and picked her up, and she wrapped her legs around his waist. His scent was driving her crazy. Intoxicating her and Genie couldn't help but feel comfort. It was the comfort she'd grown accustomed to. Comfort of the man she loved.

Nitro lifted her higher putting her back against the wall and wrapped her legs around his neck. He took her clit in his mouth and sucked on it gently. Like a puppy trying to nurse on his mama tittie. "Nitroooo, fuck." It had been a while since she got head like this. It had been so long since they tucked their disdain for one another and Nitro was showing out like he had a point to prove. Flicking his tongue across her pearl he filled her wetness with two fingers making Genie cum instantly. Nitro was an eater and he wasted no time consuming her juices.

He placed Genie on the floor, and tried turning her around to bend her over but Genesis had a different plan. She dropped to her knees, and slipped his pants and boxers down together letting her favorite piece of him free. It was beautiful and Genie was sure this was her last time fucking him. So she was about to suck his dick like her life depended on it. She chuckled to herself because her life really did depend on it.

Genie filled her mouth with Nitro, and savored the taste of him. She wasted no time putting him down her throat whole. Taking her two hands she twisted the base and sucked the head almost making him nut prematurely. Grabbing Genie by her hair, he pulled her up and led her to a chair that they had in the room. Sitting down on the chair, Nitro pulled Genie down on top of him and she rode him nice and slow. Genie made sure Nitro felt her, clenching her walls around him came up slow and dropped back down hard.

"Damn ma, you showing out." Nitro eyes were rolling into the back of his head. *I got his ass right where I want him.* Genie smirked to herself as she worked her hips like a dancehall queen. She wanted to put it on him so good that he would fall in love.

Nitro didn't give a fuck that he was fucking the enemies daughter. The way Genesis showed her sexual talents she was turning him to her bitch and he was here for it. "Fuck, slow down G."

Genie kissed him to shut him up and continued to bounce that ass on him. The feeling she was feeling was God sent. Genie wanted this nut more than she wanted her life at this point. Nitro's dick was her kryptonite. Finally at her peak, she came all over Nitro and she felt Nitro shoot all of his kids in her. Leaning into him she played like she was going to sleep so her plan could work. Stroking Genie's hair, Nitro eyes closed as he basked in the moment with her. This was the last moment between them. The nut that Genie pulled outta him, had him spent. The warmness of Genie's body heat as she laid onto him was like a spell. Genie still had him wrapped in her pussy and she wasn't rising. Genie hugged him tightly and played in his dreads. It was their thing. They played in one another's hair after rounds. But one round had been enough.

The slight hum that fell through Nitro's lips were like music to Genie's ears. She put the beast to sleep. And she wasn't trying to wake him up.

She slowly slid off of him holding her breath as she released his piece from her grip. She snatched her bloody shirt up from the ground and grabbed her dirty shorts. Genie had never gotten dressed so quickly. She tiptoed over to Nitro's pants and took his keys out of his pockets quietly.

Genie's heart rate tripled as she dashed for the door. She was sure she was holding her breath with every movement and she didn't care. She wouldn't breathe until she was out of there because if he got caught she was sure she would be dead.

Her hands shook as she quietly unlocked the door. *Gracias, dios.* She silently thanked the man above as she tiptoed out the door. She locked the door back and made it out the building straight to Nitro's car. Tears filled Genies eyes as she pulled off. She didn't dare look back as she made her way to her family. The Vado family had to pay. They were going to pay. She would make sure of it.

***

The yellow pillows, yellow wall, and yellow comforter were dulled by Cher's mood. She'd went from grieving in her bedroom to grieving in Chasity's room. She'd thought the room would bring her a sense of peace. Bring her closer to her daughter but it didn't. Being in Chas's room did nothing but bring tears to Cher's eyes. Tears of misery, of pain, of loss. The pain in her chest was tight and her nose was now stopped up. The stuffiness she'd brought into the room caused her to try breathing through her mouth but Cher was a wreck. She sobbed into Chasity's pillow as she laid in a fetal position. She couldn't believe it. Her baby was really gone. They'd hurried her funeral and she hadn't even realized. Like a machine Cher was on autopilot. Everything was a blur. The only thing that was clear was Chasity wasn't around.

Cher had always been top of class and for the first time she knew what it felt like to be a failure. To fail at nurturing and protecting life. *How did I let this happen. She'd went to get something to drink.* Chasity's death was tearing Cher to shreds day by day. The pain never lessened. Just worsened and Cher was like a zombie.

"I'm so sorry baby. I should have protected you. I should have protected you!" Cher cried as she hit the pillow wildly. She was sure that her daughter had taken a peace of her with her because Cher felt death lingering near. It was the only thing to make the pain stop. But she had two beautiful baby boys she had to nurture. The fear of failing at being their mother made her stomach twist in knots.

"Baby mi kno how yuh feel." Rich consoled her as he climbed into the bed with Cher. He pulled her onto his chest. His guilt already weighed on it and with Cher's dead weight added Rich could feel the pressure. The same pressure that he was sure the heart felt when it cracked. His was done right down the middle and the small piece that was holding up was fighting for Cher. Guilt was crawling through his veins and made him wanna end it all. A father was supposed to protect their child and he'd led his into harm's way. Although he hadn't started the situation Rich's guilt of being in the game was to blame. Kill had spoken to him for so many day, nights, telling him that he didn't want a kid until he was out of the game. Rich hadn't understood why. He could never let the game control his household. But it did. His daughter had died as a casualty. And that shit broke Rich apart. Cher's cries were taunting him. But he still laid there. He wasn't the best husband and his wife needed him more than ever. He had to be present, for her. But when Cher's head rose off his chest Rich was confused.

She sat up with her hair wild, puffy eyes, and snotty nose as she shook her head from side to side in disapproval. "She's supposed to be here Rich." Her lip trembled as she cried. She placed her hand over her mouth to stifle the sound.

"I need time. I can't do this. My baby is gone because of you Badrick. What kind of father are you? What kind of mother am I to marry a man like you?" Cher's words were like daggers through the other half of his heart. Overkill. Rich's hurt displayed on his face and Cher didn't care. She wanted him to hurt forever. He'd hurt her forever. She was sure the pain of losing a child would never cease and she hoped Rich never got a good night's rest.

"Baby just let me-"

"Go Rich, just please go!" Cher cried as her eyes pooled with emotion again.

Rich climbed from the bed feeling like he'd lost his own life. Cher was always so strong and he'd finally broken her. The bitches didn't matter to her as long as he kept them at a respectable distance. But this had hit too close to home. To her womb and it was

unforgettable. *She don't wan me no more.*

Chapter 15

Carson's hand with a knife was lethal. In every aspect. It was his favorite choice of death and his favorite part of cooking. Cutting green and red peppers for his ackee and saltfish dish. It was one of his favorite meals and the only thing that could lift his full spirit at the moment. Chas's death was paining him. Everyday he felt like he could've been a little quicker and pushed her out of the way. He played a million different scenarios in his mind that could've kept her alive. Take a bullet for her. But he was just a little too slow and it made him feel slightly defeated. But as he watched his hands move swiftly dicing onions he felt fast. He was in his head. He slid his peppers into his saucepan adding his spices to it before he played Crazy Story by King Von.

A knock at the door stole his attention and his brows piqued up in slight interest. Troi was at work, his brothers always announced when they were coming over and Sonny's mind went into overdrive.

He gripped the knife and headed towards the door. Looking through the peephole a smile graced his lips as he swung the door open. It was his favorite girl in the world. Somehow he and Troi had fit like two pieces to a puzzle. They vibed and Troi mellowed him out. He liked how he felt when he was with her. She brought out a softer side of him. Brightened the dull bulb in his heart. "You missed me?" She asked with a knowing smile. She could tell he was in his head and she'd popped up at the perfect time. The wrinkle in his forehead was proof.

He finessed his goatee with a smile while pulling her into him. "I missed you, you finally quit?" He asked, rolling his eyes as he pulled the hair tie from her locs, letting them down.
Her laughter answered his question and he shook his head as he led the way. "It smells in good here. What you cooking? Why didn't I know you could cook?"

"Ackee and Saltfish and because you don't give me a reason too. We eat out so much all the food I had went bad."

"Well now that I know you ChefBoyard Sonny I ain't cooking no more and we gon save some money." She walked over to the stove and picked up the paddle tasting it. Troi's eyes bulged in surprise because Sonny didn't need a woman to cook for him. He had this shit down pack.

"I guess that mean we be fucking more than we be talking," Sonny chuckled slapping her ass, for the first time he twisted his dreads in uneasiness. He was fully comfortable around Troi and would live in her skin if he could. But they hadn't done the basics. He was feeling a bit amateurish.

"Well tonight we gon be doin a whole lot of talking. It's crazy that I been in your face for four months and didn't know you could throw down. From now on you cooking for me."

"Alright, I ain't got no problem with that." Troi blushed as she took a seat on the barstool while watching him concentrate on his meal at hand. She was surprised at how Sonny moved around the kitchen. She'd never seen him this tranquil. Like he was doing something that he found comfort in.

After four months of being together Sonny had Troi wrapped around his finger, and she had him wrapped around hers. Sex was their favorite form of communication and Troi didn't mind. But somehow watching him cook she realized she didn't know much about him. Shit he'd hit the nail on the head. They fucked more than they talked and it had never dawned on her.

"I still can't believe I didn't know you could cook."

"I grew up in my family's restaurant. Because my parents died when I was a baby. Rich raised us. When he met Cher she basically raised me. Had me in the kitchen with her everyday."

"And she be throwing down in that restaurant so I know you know how to cook cook now." Sonny smirked realizing that Troi wasn't temporary. She'd been around since the day he'd took her from her ex and she'd never gone back. Most of the time they flirted which turned into fucking.

They were past the stage of just fuck buddies. He was engulfed in her no ifs, ands, or buts. He hadn't kicked her to the curb. Troi proved to not need him and it made Sonny want her more. She refused to quit her job because she didn't want to depend on no man. She didn't call out of work to lay up. Troi was about her business and that was a first for a woman in Sonny's life. He'd even cut down his top ten. He now had a starting 5 and Troi took up eighty percent of his time not leaving much for the others. She was it so there was no need to hold back anymore.

"What you wanna know about me?" He asked as he grabbed a bottle of Dusse. Troi's brows scrunched up as she shook her head from side to side.

"Unh unh, put that down. I brought wine. It makes you nicer. One minute I'll be driving the boat and the next I'll be riding the D. So no,"

Sonny chuckled at her assumption knowing she was right. He threw his hand up in defeat not daring to argue. What she was asking of him wasn't out of the ordinary. For once he didn't mind giving in to a woman. He grabbed two glasses and set them on the counter.

"You don't have any wine glasses?"Sonny gave her a knowing look and Troi giggled knowing she was pushing it. He wasn't a wine drinking nigga. But for her he would. She was pulling at a playas heart strings and she marveled in it. "Why do you get set off so easily?"

"Damn, you sure we don't need the Dusse?"

"What you can't take a little pressure sober?" Troi challenged him, wanting to know what he was avoiding. It was as if her question pushed a button. And she wanted to know which one.

Sonny took a seat across from her and filled his glass to the rim. "I was diagnosed with IED disorder,"

"Intermittent explosive disorder," Troi's cut him off. It was now Sonny's turn to be surprised. "My mom was a nurse. My dad was diagnosed with it. Do you take your mood stabilizers?"

Sonny shook his head shrugging the idea off. "I'm not into taking drugs. My weed calms me down."

"But your drinking is filled with rage."

"I'm working on it," he told her, holding up the glass of wine before gulping it down. "Shit taste like juice." He shook his head from side to side. Troi laughed. "But I saw something. When you brought up your parents. Your glow dimmed for the second."

"My dad was abusive. Anytime he wasn't taking his pills he would drink. And he would get mean. He beat my mother. He would beat her so bad I'd have to help her to the bed. And whenever he'd ask me to grab him a glass of water, I'd crush his pill, mix it in his water and he'd drink it. I would try to get him a glass of water everyday to make it stop. It worked."

Sonny's eyes filled with surprise. He hadn't expected for Troi to just lay it all out there. To hear her voice shaking and the lone tear that slipped her eye he could tell she'd been scared. "You scared of me?" He asked her the only question that came to mind.

"Before you sat at the bar I was. I always saw you lashing out. But when you approached me you weren't all that bad." She tried lightening the mood. She didn't want to dampen their spirits. She didn't want to get caught up in only her past trauma. She wanted the two of them to give one another a glimpse of why they were the person they were. And they were off to a good start. "Don't be scared of me. There's enough people out there scared of me and you're the one person I don't want to be scared. I'm never gonna hurt you."

Troi nodded believing every single word. She held onto them and cherished them and hoped that he meant them. Because she was so wrapped up in him if he did something to her it would take the breath from her.

She filled both their glasses halfway and smirked holding it up. "To getting to know one another." Sonny nodded and placed his glass to hers.

"To catching a vibe, the Dusse coming out after this."

***

Genie sat in her car in disbelief. She still couldn't believe that she and Nitro had gone half on a baby. The sonogram in her hand made it real. At four months pregnant a part of Genie was happy, knowing that their baby would be her pride and joy. She was sure when she told Nitro they would ride off into the sunset. Be the family that fate had made them. There was so much tension between their families that she feared telling anyone. But she had hope. That this baby would probably mend their families together. Just as she started her car ready to leave, her eyes roamed across the street. They sparked with interest. In broad daylight Nitro and the bitch she almost fought was walking hand in hand, into the ice cream parlor across the street from her doctors office. Her face went red and she began feeling hot. *Here I am carrying this nigga baby, and he parading this bitch around town.* He didn't know the truth but still, Genie's rage and hormones were taking over.

She laid her head onto the steering wheel, and weighed her pros and cons. *I could go over there and cause a scene or I could leave and act like I never seen them.* Genid tried convincing herself but her pride wouldn't let her. *It wouldn't be right if he didn't know about his baby.* She smirked to herself then drove across the street and got out of her car. She hadn't seen or heard from him in months and watching him give Imani all of his attention made her skin crawl. Genie knew all she had to do was walk in the room and he would see her. *I think I want some ice cream.* "Baby Nitro wants ice cream." She mumbled to herself.

When Genie walked in the building and Nitro didn't spot her right away she scrunched her face up in confusion. *Why the fuck don't he see me?*

Nitro and Imani sat at a picnic table eating ice cream, even though it was fall the sun was still out in Atlanta and temperature was perfect. Genie scoffed ready to ruin their lil date. They looked so happy and it made her sick to her stomach. She was ready to ruin their little fantasy.

Nitro spotted Genie walking towards them and froze. She was sporting a tight adidas shirt, adida leggings and some adida shoes, but that wasn't what he was paying attention to. His eyes were glued to her little belly stretching her shirt. "Nah, she can't be." Nitro meant to say that internally. Imani's brows arched together in confusion. Once the words left his mouth Genie was standing behind Imani.

She placed her hand on her stomach, smiling at Nitro. "Long time no see old friend." Genie stood there glowing and Imani was enraged by this point. This bitch was standing here, in her face rubbing her belly and talking to her fucking man.

Everyone could see the bitch was pregnant and Imani prayed it wasn't Nitro's. She hadn't signed up for baby mama drama and from her one encounter with Genie the bitch was nothing but drama. *Did he really have a baby on me?* Imani's mind raced as she kept her poker face. She'd let Genie see her sweat once and refused to let it happen again. Nitro had some explaining to do.

"Genie, what the fuck is this?" He finally found his voice. His eyes never left her belly. To one it may have looked like she ate a little too much, but Nitro knew Genie's body. It wasn't a pudge from eating.

"Oh this?" Genie rubbed her belly again, this time locking eyes with Imani to taunt her.

"Yes bitch, that." Imani stood up ready to bash Genie's head into the table they were at. Genie didn't back down and she stood her ground ready for Imani to pop off. Her hand slid into her purse so she could have easy access to her .45. Genie's only instinct was protecting her and her baby. Especially after being caught lacking by the Vado's she was prepared this time. *Imma leave this bitch slump if she take another step.*

"Nah, y'all chill. Genie what's going on?" Nitro pulled Imani near him so she wouldn't pop off on Genie. He could feel his girl ticking like a time bomb. Genie tried handing Nitro the sonogram but Imani snatched it out of her hand,

"Nitro, tell me you didn't go and get this bitch pregnant." Imani's eyes started to fill up with tears but she shook it off because the last thing she wanted was to cry in front of Genie.

"Yup, I'm pregnant and it's your baby Nitro. The last time we were together, you remember don't you? That time I put you to sleep." Genie was now taunting Nitro. Imani might not have known what she was talking about but Nitro remembered. When she fucked him to sleep, locked him in the room and took his car. The thought alone had Nitro ready to kill her. *I still ain't get my muhfucking car back.*

"How the fuck do I know this my baby, I ain't seen you in four months G." He couldn't wrap his head around having a baby with a fucking DeLeon. His brothers were going to beat his ass if they knew this.

"Exactly it's been four months. You didn't pull out remember? Look at the sonogram and you'll see for yourself." Taking the sonogram from Imani, Nitro looked at it and sure enough the time matched up to when this crazy bitch locked him in the basement.

"Nitro, if this ya baby, I promise you I'm about to hurt you right here right now." Imani popped him in the back of his head like he was a child. Genie, didn't like that one bit. She was possessive and somehow in the back of her mind she believed Nitro was hers. That he would come home after this news. Imani was overstepping, putting her hands on him and Genie was ready to let her have it.

"Bitch don't put your hands on him."

"What the fuck you gone do about it?" Imani barked in her face. Every part of her wanted to drag Genie up and down the ice cream parlor but she wasn't trying to go to jail. She was done talking, because the more she talked the more upset she got. Imani tried walking around Nitro but he grabbed her by her waist and pulled her into his lap

"Ma chill, for me please." He whispered in her ear. His head was starting to hurt. He and Imani were doing good and now Genie ass was back on some bullshit.

Watching Nitro comfort Imani, made tears fall down Genie's face. Her hormones and emotions were everywhere. This was how Nitro was supposed to be with her, even if she hated his guts he was supposed to be there and comfort her. *I'm carrying his damn baby.* It was the only validation Genie had and the weight she thought it held was imaginary.

"Genie just leave, I'll get with you." Imani moved from his grip and began to walk towards the car. If she didn't, she'd be in cuffs and Genie's and Nitro's baby would be dead. The thought didn't seem too bad but Imani knew it wasn't her place. Nitro had fucked up and now they had to figure out what the fuck was next.

"NITRO, BRING YO ASS ON!" Imani yelled from the car. Looking at Genie one more time he promised to call her and walked towards his pissed off girlfriend.

Tears fell from Genie's eyes as Nitro walked away from her. One thing about them tables was they always turned. Now Genie's feelings were hurt and Nitro was about to pay for it. Her and her

baby came second to no fucking one.

Chapter 16

"I'm so happy we're finally able to spend some time together, I missed you so much Richy." Rich was laid out on the couch laying in Missy's lap. This was the only peace he had since Chas died. His wife wanted nothing to do with him and his brothers were off doing their own thing. Rich knew it was fucked up but Missy was his safe place right now. Her hands caressing his scalp like she was massaging his thoughts eased him.

"Mi tuh, mi missed yuh." He reached up and grabbed her by the neck pulling her head down to kiss her. Everything he would've been doing with Cher he did with Missy. She was quite the replacement. Going above and beyond to make sure he was straight and he appreciated it. That kiss alone took Missy breath away, she needed that reassurance more than she needed her next breath.

"When are you going to leave her Richy, you promised me that it would be me and you." She asked the minute she came up for breath. Missy was so in love with Rich that it hurt her. Rich leaving Cher was all that she wanted. She wanted to be able to call Rich hers, she wanted to be the one to carry his babies and live in that big mansion that Cher was living in. In other words she wanted Cher's life and would never say it. Just inquire about all the things Cher had.

"Mi working towards it. Mi have too much going on right now." Sitting up on the couch Rich put his head in his hands. The last couple months had been rough on him. He was missing his daughter, his brothers were in their own world and his wife was… shit, his wife didn't want shit to do with him. But still Rich couldn't leave her alone.

Missy wanted something he couldn't offer but how could Rich tell her that. He fed her dreams and lies, he was never leaving his wife for her. Even with the disconnect between them. She was the only other person who experienced the pain he'd endured from Chas's death. The only one who truly knew how he felt.

"You've been saying that for years. When is it going to be me, when am I going to be number one." Straddling him, she put her hands on his face and made him look her in the eyes. "Tell me you love me."

As she stared into Rich eyes, Missy didn't see what she wanted to see. She didn't see the love she wanted Rich to have for her. He didn't look at her the way he looked at his wife but that didn't stop her from having hope. Missy had been riding with Rich for so long that no one, not even Rich could convince her that he didn't love her. In her mind, Rich loved her more than he loved Cher. He just concealed it so well like he'd done her for years that it wasn't visible. But she felt it. What they shared was real in her mind and the only person in their way was Cher.

The ringing of the door bell, stopped their intense stare and Missy lifted herself off him. "This conversation is not over." She told him while heading towards the door.

When she opened it, she was surprised to see Cher standing on the other side.

"Are you going to let me in sister wife?" Cher didn't wait for Missy to invite her in, she walked straight into the home like she owned it, making sure to mug her with each step she took. Shit, technically if her husband purchased it she did own this bitch.

Closing the door behind them, Missy followed behind Cher excited to see how shit was about to play out. Hopefully Cher would leave Rich and finally he could be with her.

"Damn, you look real cozy. Like you're right at home or something. And I know yo ass bought this shit cause that broke hoe ain't got it." Rich jumped up at the sound of his wife's voice, he was stuck. Like a deer in headlights he wasn't prepared. *Why di fuck is Cher here? How she know where Missy live?*

"What cat got your tongue?" Cher stood in front of Rich because by now he was off the couch and standing up.

She stared at him in disgust. He was real comfortable. He was sitting there without a shirt on, a pair of boxers and the muthafucka had a beer resting on the table like he was king around this bitch.

With her 6 inch heels on Cher still wasn't as tall as her husband but she looked at him like he was short. Standing in front of him she meant business and she wasn't leaving there with unanswered questions.

"Cher wat yuh doing here?" Rich asked the only question in his mind. It was a dumb question, and the look on Cher's face said it.

"What I'm doing here. No Rich, what the fuck you doing here!? Is this where you've been for a week? While I'm home taking care of your fucking kids! This is where you want to be Rich? Because if it is, I will have yo shit boxed up and mailed to you." Cher exploded like a volcano. This was her last straw. Rich couldn't continue playing her like a dummy. She wasn't backing down, she was furious and scorned.

"It take for mi tuh leaf, fi yuh to notice mi. How di fuck yuh tink mi feel. Mi fucking wife walking round ignoring me."

Cher stepped back and looked at her husband. Broken and upset, how could he try to flip this on her when she was nothing but loyal to him.

"You brought everything on yourself, you're not gon ever change, Rich. It's best to just leave this here." Cher was defeated, all she wanted was Rich out her life for good.

"Yeah how bout y'all just forget it. Now you can be with me Rich, ain't that what you was just telling me? You're going to leave her for me." Missy finally spoke up. Watching Rich and Cher was like an episode of Days of our Lives and it was time for her to make her grand entrance. She walked over to Rich standing beside him. Missy clung to his arm rubbing it gently causing Rich to move from her grasp. "Tell her Rich. Tell her that you're leaving her for me."

"Yeah Rich, tell me. Tell me that you leaving. I dare you" Cher set her purse down ready for the wrong words to come out of Rich mouth. She didn't want his sorry ass anyways. It was just the audacity that he'd been telling his mistress he was leaving like he wasn't the cause of their family falling apart. Like he wasn't the reason her baby was gone. Cher was borderline over the edge and ready to set shit the fuck off.

"Cher, let's chat bout dis elsewhere. Mi will meet yuh at home." Rich tried de-escalating the problem. He knew his wife and he knew she wouldn't continue to take Missy popping off at her. Missy was playing a game that Cher wasn't too good at. Cher was his wife for a reason. The tiger in her she concealed very well. But Rich could tell his lady was at her breaking point.

"No, you're going to tell her now! Richy tell her that you're leaving her for me. Let her go Richy and it'll be me and you forever."

BANG!

Missy was so caught up in what she was trying to do while Rich was trained on trying to get her to shut the fuck up that neither one saw the gun that Cher pulled from her waistband. Missy landed on the floor gasping for the air that she desperately needed. Cher showed no ounce of regret from what she'd done. She didn't care. This woman disrespected her one to many times, and Rich had allowed her. She'd made it clear to him to keep his bitches on a leash but it was clear Missy was a stray. Cher was a Vado not by blood but a Vado she definitely was. She walked over to Missy and pulled the trigger once more letting a shot off into her head, her husband taught her to never leave a job unfinished.

Rushing over to Missy, Rich kneeled and looked at his wife with a pain that she knew all too well. He loved her, he actually loved this bitch and it was at this point the Cher knew she had to go. She could bear her husband cheating on her, but the pain in his eyes watching Missy take her last breath showed love. The love he was only supposed to have for her. Cher walked away from the scene and didn't look back. Not even when she heard Rich calling out for her.

"CHER!"

"CHER!" Rich closed Missy eyes and rushed behind his wife, but it was too late. Cher was already gone and Rich had to figure out what he was about to do with the dead body of his mistress.

***

"Nigga, that scale is an ounce over." Kill scolded Kaylin as he took a piece of the Kings Bread marijuana lightening the scale.

Weed filled the air, the table, and bags. He was working and Kay was right beside him like she always was.

"Boy you so damn petty," Kaylin giggled, rolling her eyes as she dumped the weed off the scale into a bag.

"Nah, if you go an ounce over everytime that shit add up. That's a bag that a nigga could be smoking, spending, investing, or profiting. I'm not taking no shorts." He schooled her. "Move over. Now a nigga gotta watch you, cause you over here being Santa.

"Boy fuck you," Kaylin giggled mushing him as she snatched the blunt from his lips placing it onto hers. "I thought you ain't supposed to smoke the product,"

"I don't smoke my product. I bought my product ma."

Kaylin shook her head from side to side as she kicked her feet up on the table blowing into the air. *He better than me. One of a kind.* Kaylin stared at him with admiration. Kill concentrated on placing the weed onto the scale. He had a ton of weed to distribute to each city. They'd allowed their mourning to get the best of them and the streets had dried up right under their nose. They left time and space for other rookies to pull up to Georgia and try to finesse their way onto the Vados territory. After making a few examples out of a few out of town cats, it was time to get back on their grind. In full force.

He poured his everything into working. He reinforced his energy into the streets not leaving much time for anyone. Kaylin popped in and out whenever she wanted. The ringing of his phone on the table caused her to sit up and pick it up. Kill's concentration remained. Kaylin had seen every nude, text, sex tape, and dm in his phone. He didn't hide any part of himself from her. "It's yo sister in law" she put quotes around the word rolling her eyes back.

Kill finally turned his attention to her answering the phone. "Wassup."

"Akiel, you better help me get my shit out of this house. Or imma kill this motherfucker! I will lay that bitch ass nigga in the dirt! I did it to his bitch and I should've bodied his ass too!" Cher screamed into the phone. She was distraught and it made Kill's heart rate speed up. He stood up in his seat and looked over at Kaylin. Kill had known the moment would come, the day where he'd have to deal with being in the middle of the two of them. He hadn't known how soon it would come. He'd kept his distance from Cher not wanting anyone else to make the assumption. But now here he was with Kaylin handling business and Cher was on his line. Her threats to his brother, and what she'd said she did made him have to pick her. "KK I be back."

He could tell his words were like a punch to her gut. It didn't matter what Kaylin thought that moment. Her depiction of Kill and Cher together blurred the reality that Cher was family. He grabbed his button up yankee jersey throwing it over his wife beater. "Imma be right back. Finish bagging and I got something for you." He winked at her then headed out the door without waiting on a reply.

Kaylin's blood boiled and her heart raced. Because it was bleeding out slowly and trying to seal itself back up. The sound of Kill's tire screeching on the pavement split her in half. He was in a rush. Cher pulled rank and Kaylin's hurt returned to anger. She finished smoking the blunt as her anger brewed. The smoke she was inhaling came out of her ears.

Kaylin finally put the blunt out and dumped all of the unbagged weed into a bag. *This nigga want to play with me. Imma show him I'm the big playa.* Kaylin's temper consumed her as she went in and out of the trap to bring numerous duffle bags of weed into her trunk. With ample amount of time to change her mind and stop what she was doing Kaylin's pride wouldn't allow her to. The entitlement of being his only friend for so long was coming out of her. She came before everyone. Even Cher, and if she didn't know. Now he would.

Chapter 17

Genie still couldn't believe what transpired a week ago. Nitro played her and her baby to the side and she wasn't about to let it slide. It didn't matter how much she tried telling herself she was overreacting. She was still upset. Genie's ego and pride was bruised and she just wanted to make Nitro feel the same way. Looking in the mirror, she realized it was the entitlement that made her so upset. She was carrying his baby, his baby mama and he'd left her for the next bitch.

The tears rolling down her face smeared her makeup making her look a hot mess. This rejection wasn't supposed to hurt this bad because she wasn't supposed to even be worried about Nitro.

Seeing Imani with Nitro is what sparked her interest a little more than it should have. She hated to feel like she lost Nitro to another woman, even if Imani had him first. "You're going to be okay Genie. You're a DeLeon we don't cry over spilt milk." She coached herself in the mirror. She sat on her bed when she realized her pep talk wasn't working. Genie couldn't help but think that she was wrong when she begged her father to squash the beef between the two families. *He would've been dead if I didn't stop Papi. I saved him and his family and he played me for that bitch.*

"Fuck it, I got something for his ass." Jumping off her bed, Genie slid her Gucci flops on, grabbed her keys and purse and rushed out the front door. Her mind was racing a million miles per hour, she had the perfect idea. Genie wanted Nitro to hurt like she'd been hurting and he was about to feel every pain he brought to her.

It took her no time to pull up to her fathers house. She climbed out of the car and rushed inside the house and straight to her fathers den.

"Papi? Papi? Are you in here." Genie opened the door and her father was on his computer working on something but she didn't care. She had something to tell him and she needed to tell him now. Forcing tears down her face, she was playing this role well. She'd put an entire plan together in her mind on how she'd get Nitro back.

Alejandro stopped all he was doing and focused on his baby girl who was breaking down in front of him. "Genie habla conmigo nena.(Genie what's wrong talk to me baby girl) Alejandro rose from his seat and led her to the couch. His baby was hurting and he was ready to go to war with somebody.

"Papi, he-he-he raped me." Genie buried her face in her father's neck and cried until her face was red as a cherry. She was crying like she was actually raped, crying like she was reliving this moment that never happened.

"Who raped you Genie. Quien cono te violo. (Who the fuck raped you)". By now steam coming out Alejandro's ears as he stood up. No one was bold enough to lay a fucking hand on his daughter and violate her in the most fucked up way. "Genesis answer me!"

"Nitro, it was Nitro Vado papi." Alejandro stopped pacing the floor upon hearing the name. He couldnt win for losing with the fucking Vado family. They were coming for blood. They'd violated. The thought of the torture his daughter had endured made his stomach turn.

"A fucking Vado." Alejandro laughed to keep from crying. This was the worst news anyone had ever told him. It was his job to protect his daughter, and this bitch ass nigga violated her.

"Papi, I'm, I'm." She couldn't finish her sentence so she lifted up the shirt she was wearing to show her dad her belly. The baby that she was carrying inside her, the baby that she and Nitro made together. The baby of the person who *raped* her. The look on her fathers face let her know her mission was complete.

Alejandro couldn't stop the tears this time, his daughter was pregnant by a fucking Vado. This was karma. It had to be karma. As he sat next to his daughter Alejandro pulled her into him and sat quietly.

"I'll handle him Genie, I promise he's not getting away with this." Alejandro pulled out his phone calling Gunz letting him know that it was time to move in on Nitro. Nitro had to pay with his life, there was no other way around it. "You're staying here tonight Genie, I don't want you staying by yourself right now. Are you keeping this baby?"

"Papi, I'm four months pregnant, I'm keeping my baby." Her response should have been the first red flag for Alejandro. But all he saw was red. Nodding his head he told Genie that he'd be back a little later and walked out the door.

Once Alejandro was gone, Genie went into her room and laughed. She should have gotten a fucking grammy for the way she acted. Nitro's days were limited now and she could smile knowing that if she didn't have him neither did Imani.

Taking her sonogram out her purse she looked at it and smiled. This baby was her blessing, but his or her father had to go. She knew it was wrong but at this point she didnt give a fuck. It was them against everyone

***

The sound of dice rubbing against one another then hitting the pavement was equivalent to the sound *cha-ching* in Nitro's ear. A dice game on the corner was always a fun way to make quick money. His mind was fucked up. A baby, the thought of it gave him a headache. Warming up milk, changing diapers, and doing daddy shit, sounded okay but coparenting with a DeLeon just didn't sit right with his soul.

"Gimme my fucking money nigga," Sonny shit talked as he walked up on his brother. Lately his temper had been under control and Nitro couldn't front it was like the peace in their lives had been restored since Genie had escaped. The DeLeon's hadn't come back after them and Llanzo had made them stand down and take their loss. Once again they'd lost to the DeLeon family. The reality of Genie being a DeLeon still blew his mind just like the bomb she'd dropped. If there was one thing Genie would do every time she saw

Nitro it was blow his mind. Whether it be in bed, or on his two feet. She was full of surprises.

Nitro pulled out his wad of money slapping two bills into Sonny's hands. "I ain't tripping, my baby shower is on you," he joked, making Sonny laugh.

"When you gon tell Rich and Kill?" Sonny asked with a raised brow while chewing on a cup of ice. It was some shit Troi had him doing every time he had the urge to drink. Although he'd wanted to pour up and drink Henny straight he held it down. The news of Nitro impregnating a DeLeon had stunned him. Nitro hadn't told him Genie was his baby mama It was embarrassing. He wasn't the one who usually fucked up and this time he did. Big time. He shrugged his shoulders and took a sip of his drink while Sonny shook the dice in his hand.

"When he get here." He decided, making Sonny laugh. He looked at Nitro to see if he was serious and his expression was.

"And y'all call me the wild one. I've been cooling you been shooting the club up." Sonny threw down his dice.

"Nah nigga, you been been up Troi ass and I ain't complaining. Stay there forreal bro, you been doing good." Nitro nodded his head with a smirk on his face as he spotted Troi.

Sonny turned his head to see what had caught his brother's eye. His face frowned in disapproval as he watched Troi head towards him in a red lace bodysuit with ripped jean shorts that she kept the zipper open on. *She dressed like a fucking ho.* Sonny thought to himself as he headed towards her. "Speaking of the devil," Nitro commented already knowing that Sonny was on ten. He didn't know his words had triggered Sonny. *In that fucking red.* Her entire outfit looked like it had been painted on her. Her shorts were too short, gripping her ass tightly showing her full figure. There was little left to imagination and Sonny wasn't fond of it.

"Yo, where is your clothes?" Sonny asked her like he was truly confused.

"What you see is what you get." She smirked knowing that she'd pissed him off.

"You want to get somebody hurt out here."

"You are too, got them grey short sweats on with this crisp ass tank top, what's that Gucci shades? A fresh line up, and earrings.

I'm glad I surprised you. Cause you dressed like a fucking ho." She told him waving her finger in his face. She was provoking him and loving it. Showing him who was boss.

"We out," he told her, not wanting to further the conversation. She wasn't sitting on the block with him while he played dice around of bunch of niggas. For her he was curving fingers around his trigger and he didn't even want to get to that. He was doing good. Nitro had said it and he wanted to keep it up.

"You took your pill? Cause me coming out like this shouldn't have you mad like this."

Sonny flashed her a tight lipped smile. "I ain't mad. I was about to leave anyway." He turned to Nitro and threw a letter V up with his fingers Nitro sent his back with a head nod.

Sonny hadn't even spun fully when he heard the shots being fired. *POW POW POW POW*

His heart raced as he threw Troi down onto the floor and hopped over her. He pulled his gun out while shielding her. His heart was racing. He couldn't lose anyone else. Sonny stood from behind the car letting shots go through the glass of the car.

RATATATATTATAT

They had machine guns and were spraying. Bodies everyone around dropped and painted the floor red. When Sonny saw Nitro laid in his own paint he stopped breathing for a second. Disregarding the gunfire he rushed over to his brother. "Sonny!" Troi yelled in fear that he would be next.

The sound of tires screeching pulling from the scene allowed her to breath again. She cautiously stood up while shaking. Her ears were ringing and her heart was racing. She walked over to Sonny and the sight of him on the floor trying to keep Nitro awake broke her heart. Tears fell from his eyes, as Nitro fought for his life. "We have to call the ambulance!" Troi pulled out her phone and began dialing.

"No, call my brothers. Call them!" He rushed, keeping his eyes on Nitro.

"Denetro don't do this shit man. Don't leave me man. I can't take another loss bro." Sonny pleaded while tears cascaded his face. Tears of fear. Nitro's wide eyes showed that he was fighting to stay with him.

"Sonny, watch over my kid bro. Look out for him. My baby mother is Genie DeLeon." Nitro fought to get the words out.

Sonny's eyes widened. Nitro had really fucked up and they were after him. The news hadn't fully made its way through Sonny's ear canal as Nitro slowly closed his eyes. "They're on their way." Troi told him while kneeling beside him. She placed her hand onto Nitro's chest feeling a faint heartbeat. She ran her hand around the holes in his shirt. He'd been shot four times and blood leaked out of him.

The sound of tires screeching caused him to grab his gun again but when he saw both of his brothers hop out of the car he was like a child. Hoping that they would save the day. Save their brother because if Chas's death didn't kill him Nitro's would. He was his best friend, favorite brother and life without him was non existent.

Troi kept her hand on his wrist feeling his pulse get faint buy the second. Nitro was struggling to breathe and if she didn't help he would die. But the thought of Nitro's life in her hand and him not making it scared her. She couldn't be the one with his life in her hands. Against her better judgement she hopped into the car and placed both her hands over his chest. Sonny entered after her allowing her to work. For the first time. He allowed her help. If his brother made it he would marry her. They'd called her the devil and so quickly shit had gone left. Saving Nitro's life would make her an angel. One that Sonny wouldn't let out of his life.

"Wah di fuck happen?" Rich asked as he sped down the street.

"He got a DeLeon pregnant," Sonny said, wanting to hold his brother's secret but knowing that they needed to know. A war with the DeLeon's was always deadly. And if they weren't dealt with quickly, they would wipe out their entire bloodline.

Chapter 18

"Yo this DeLeon shit is a wrap bro. They keep coming at us and we standing back like we fucking pussy. We got money to be making and this shit been going on for too long." Kill ranted in front of his brothers fed up. He'd had a plan and he was ready to put it in action. The DeLeon's didn't play fair and neither did he. He was ready to pay soldiers to overthrow the nigga's entire kingdom.

"He got di girl pregnant, but why now? Di bitch been left. It's been four months. Dat shit nuh making sense its nuh adding up." Rich wondered. The DeLeon's had ruined his life. Since the day his daughter died he hadn't been the same again. Once Nitro let Genie escape that was it. He knew that his opportunity was taken away. The DeLeon Mafia had an army that was bigger than theirs and going toe to toe was deadly. Something he couldn't risk. "I got to be sure Cher. Gaan with the pickneys. Mi can't find them. If di DeLeon's find dem before me. Mi dead." Rich told him honestly. He needed to be 100% sure and even after he was sure he had to know where his wife and kids had gone. He couldn't keep them protected wherever they were at.

"She still ain't call you?"

"Wah mek yuh tink she wan call me? Rich scoffed as he shook his head. He'd fucked up. Cher had never killed before and Rich had watched his wife lose her mind with his very eyes. He'd poked and probed at the beast and she'd come out. Snatching souls in the process.

"I just figured she needed some time to cool off and maybe she'd let you see your youths,"

"Nah mon, yuh didn't si her. Cher nuh coming back if mi don't find her and bring her back. Mi should kill her for taking mi pickney." Rich told his brother getting upset about not having access to his kids. Cher had left him with a body to clean up and came home to nothing. No kids, no clothes, no food. She'd even gone out her way to break every mirror in the house along with the light fixtures. The safe was empty, and the ammonia and bleach combination she'd left behind told him she wanted him dead like she'd done Missy. They were done without a doubt. His kids were the only thing on his mind, seeing as though Cher had taken out his distraction.

"So we waiting on these niggas to come for us again is what your saying. They not playing fair and this shit is getting hot." Kill told him seriously.

"Yuh come up inna here like yuh ave a plan, let mi hear it"

I've already put the word out to a couple hittas about a possible hit."

"A hit, yuh got hit money? Did you find di bitch who ran off wid our shit?"

Kill clenched his jaw and lines formed in his forehead. Somehow shit had died down and began going haywire again. Rich had made Cher finally lose it, Kaylin had finally gotten tired of Kill's shit, and the DeLeon's were back guns blazing. Four months of peace was all they were granted. "Nah, I got niggas looking for her. They'll bring me her."

"You better hope they fucking do. You and Nitro fucked up big time with these bitches. Usually it's Sonny but he's been on his best behavior since he got a girl. How the bitch run off with the bread again?" Rich asked. The ringing of his phone caused him to halt Kill.

When he saw his uncle's name come across the screen he answered putting it on speaker. "Dey gwan too far. Mi wan a toe tag pon Alejandro DeLeon tonight. Whoeva can get dat dun for mi will tek ova." The line went dead just as fast as they'd answered. Rich and Kill already knew what that meant. Nitro hadn't made it. The DeLeon's had won again and now the Vado's would be repaying them a visit. The Vado's had laid too many people to rest at their hands and now it was the DeLeon's turn. Rich and Kill wanted to take out the entire bloodline, wipe out their existence. Even the baby between Genie and Nitro had to go. There was no way that a Vado and DeLeon could create a child together. Too much smoke, and blood between them couldn't allow them to coexist. It was clear the DeLeon's were plying for keep and after getting the go from Llanzo. Rich and Kill were ready to end it all once and for all.

***

The ride back to Troi"s house was quiet. Sonny and Troi were in their own thoughts. Troi couldn't help the hurt she felt for Sonny. Him not being himself, the Sonny that she knew pained her. Sonny had witnessed his brother get gunned downed while he was standing right there. It was like a repeated nightmare because he'd been right there for Chasity's death too. Reaching over Troi grabbed Sonny's hand and gave it a squeeze so he knew he wasn't alone. Looking away from the road, Sonny gave Troi a weak smile because that was all he could muster. Sonny's mind was only on Nitro, he wasn't the type of man that prayed but he was praying to God that Nitro pulled through. The Vado brothers would never be the same if Nitro wasn't here. *God please watch over my bro. Heal him, don't let him die on me. I won't be able to take it.* His prayer ended as he pulled up to Troi's house. He sat in his seat waiting for Troi to get out of the car.

"Why don't you come in for a second, you don't need to be driving alone while you feeling like this." Troi tried to convince him. She wasn't getting out of the car without Sonny going with her.

"I just need some time to myself right now, ma." The look in Sonny's eyes told Troi something different and she didn't like what they were saying. They were dark, low, and full of venom. It was a look that scared her. He turned his eyes away from her as he picked up on her body tensing up. He saw the fear he sent through her and it pained him.

"Sonny look at me." He stayed looking out the windshield, ignoring her request. "Carson look at me now!" Troi yelled, and he slowly turned his head to look at her. The pain behind his eyes was deadly. Troi wanted to take it away. It was something that she needed to take away. She knew that look far too well, it was the same look Sonny gave her ex boyfriend. The look of pain mixed with anger made him feel ready to kill someone. Sonny was ready to murder any and everybody and Troi didnt want that for him. He needed to be in the house with her, he needed his brothers but Kill and Rich were the last people on his mind.

"Troi...baby." Sonny put his head on his hands and took a deep breath before he finished his sentence. He wasn't used to having to answer to a female, all of this was new to him. He didn't want to hurt Troi but she was nagging him right now. "I need to be alone, I don't need to be around no one right now. You don't know the thoughts going through my mind right now, you never seen this side of me and I don't want you to. I don't need to be around you right now ma. Fuck!" Sonny's outburst caught Troi off guard but that didn't make her back down. Sonny was her nigga and she didnt care if he didnt want to be around her, he was about to hear what she had to say.

"Carson, lower your voice when you talk to me. I understand you hurting but I don't need you to get hurt." Tears began to fall out Troi's eyes, these few months that she'd been with Sonny, brought out something that she never felt before. She understood where he was coming from, he wanted revenge for his brother but Troi needed him. She needed him to think straight and to be here for her. "What about me Sonny, I just watched your brother get gunned down too. I need you here with me. What if they come back to finish the job and this my last time seeing you Carson." Troi was trying to say anything that would make Sonny stay with her. She wasn't worried about anyone gunning Sonny down because she knew her nigga could handle himself. Only thing Troi didn't want was for Sonny to move off of emotions, she needed him to have a clear head.

"Troi, get out. Please get out my car." Sonny told her just above a whisper.

"No, I'm not leaving." She back in her seat, and folded her arms and pouted like a child.

"What the fuck Troi. What I gotta do to make you get out my car so I can leave. I'm okay ma, I promise I am. What do you want me to do, what you want me to say."

"I want you to stay here! That's what the fuck I want Sonny."

"I don't have time for this shit Troi. I don't have no time at all ma. Please go in the house. I promise you I'm not going to do anything, I just need some time and space to clear my mind ma. I need to be alone." Troi's yelling, added to Sonny's headache. His thoughts had pounded on the inside of his head making the throbbing painful.

"If I get out this car Sonny, I'm done. If you drive away in this car. I am done!" She yelled the words hoping they'd register in his head. She was pulling the last string she had. Troi silently prayed that Sonny would walk into her home with her for the night.

She got the shock of her life when Sonny hit the locks on his car signaling her exit. Troi sighed as she opened the door and got out the car.

"Dont fucking call me! If they fucking kill you I'll never forgive you. I'll hate you." She told him finally walking away.

He watched her walk into the house, then shook his head before driving off. He had one destination in his mind. The only place he could clear his mind at. He would call Troi when she calmed down a little and his mind was clear.

Chapter 19

He picked up the old dead flowers at the grave and switched them out with the fresh ones he'd bought. Alejandro kneel onto one knee and shook his head from side to side. "Amoi, we share a grandchild. And I don't know if I should be happy or pissed. But right now I'm fucked up. What he did was fucked up." Alejandro's eyes closed as he bowed his head. He placed his hand over her tombstone. Wanting to feel closer to her. The woman he loved had lost her life over him, and he somehow felt like this was his karma.

"Alejandro I'm pregnant," Amoi whispered to him as Dajuan went off to use the bathroom. Lately he'd been hounding her like a dog. Tightening the leash around her neck not allowing her to breathe. Her woman's intuition was high and she knew Dajuan had found out. This was the first moment she'd had away from him in weeks and fear was sitting at the brim of her eyes.

"Are you gonna leave him ma? Cause if not just kill it." Alejandro told her sourly. He was tired of the games. Amoi had played him like a yo-yo for two years. And she told him everytime they were together she wouldn't leave Dajuan for him.

"I'll leave him. I think he knows there's somebody. He's going to kill me if he finds out." The fear was evident in her tone and as much as Alejandro wanted to keep his act. He couldn't. Their time was limited. Dajuan would be heading towards them soon.

"I'll have my men pick up your kids. All you gotta do is stay here."

"Yuh ready fi get back tuh bizniz?" Dajuan reentered the room with a smile on his face. The sight of him caused the blood to drain in Amoi's body. A smile like that from a man like Dajuan was only evil. Dajuan didn't smile for anyone. Not for his kids, not for his wife, and not for his business partners. The two had been doing business for a little over two years. Dajuan Vado supplied Alejandro DeLeon the finest strains of weed straight from Jamaica. DaJuan had the best shit and the entire south came to him for supply.

Dajuan wrapped his arm around his wife's waist leading her to the couch. He could feel her trembling with every step and his grip on her tightened making her wince. Alejandro sat across from the couple his face hot and it showed.

Dajuan's happiness was out of the ordinary and unpredictable. At a time where Amoi was panicking he was cool as ice. "I asked to meet with you because I'm thinking about expanding in the pill business. Everybody knows that for pills you are the man."

"How much you trying to get, and where do you plan on selling them? Georgia is taken care of."

"I'm looking for a fair exchange in products. I'll be sending it back home."

Amoi watched as the two men interacted and her mind went wild. Her eyes stayed glued to Alejandro. She was pleading without her words and although he kept his eyes on DaJuan he could feel her begging. He was trying to keep his cool while stalling a little bit but it was but so much stalling he could do. Once they were done negotiating both men stood up and Amoi followed. She watched as they shook hands. It was like a kiss of death for her. She was caught in between two business partners and although Alejandro said he'd save her. She'd just watched him make another deal with the devil. It was like her breathing stopped and she was trying to catch her breath again. But Dajuan didn't allow her. The minute he retracted his right hand back he swiftly used his left to pull out his pocket knife going across Amoi's neck with it.

Her eyes widened in fear as she grabbed her neck knowing that her life was coming to an end. Blood leaked out of her neck like a faulty sink. Her life was coming to an end quickly and she didn't even have a chance to say her last words, tell her children she loved them.

"Noooo!" Alejandro yelled in horror as he watched Amoi fall back onto the couch. She was gone, she'd only had a few seconds and they were done. The child they created was gone. Dajuan had taken a woman and a child from him and the only thing Alejandro could do was settle the score. He pulled out his gun emptying his clip in Dajuan. He filled him up with holes, and still Dajuan went down with a smirk. Like he'd been prepared to lose his life.

Dajuan had fooled Amoi and Alejandro, and that alone made his rest peaceful.

"I should've helped you ma. My ego allowed that shit to happen." Alejandro confessed. A tear fell from his eye watering the dirt beneath him. "I'm so sorry Amoi." Alejandro said one last time as he stood to his feet. His sorry was for a number of things. Sorry for not saving her, sorry for not saving their child, sorry for being her demise, and sorry for sending her child to be with her. Sorry wasn't enough but it was all Alejandro had to give his dead lover. Only the two of them knew how real what they shared was. And the guilt of her life on his hands had been the only reason he'd taken it easy on her boys. But they had violated. They were a product of their father and Alejandro was ready to send them all flying high.

"You shouldn't have come here," a voice said from behind him. Before Alejandro could move an inch the sharp steel went across his neck giving him de ja vu. Except this time, his life was slipping. Quicker than Amoi's. The right amount of pressure had been applied to his neck taking his life instantly. Amoi, the women he loved had been his karma. She'd lost her life over him and Alejandro had lost his over her. Visiting her had cost him his life.

Sonny watched as Alejandro dropped to the ground and for once he felt relief. But confusion plagued him afterwards. *What the fuck was that nigga doing here?* He thought to himself as he stared at his mother's tombstone. Alejandro's blood painted her tombstone and the peace that Sonny sought being there vanished. He stepped over Alejandro's body and kneeled before his mother. The queen. The one he hadn't had much time with and he cried. His life felt like it was spiraling and being at Amoi's grave was the only time he felt closest to her. Right now he needed her, but with a dead Alejandro beside him he felt like he needed answers.

"Mama, what is going on. What was he doing here?" Sonny sat in the spot where Alejandro was previously sitting. The pain in his heart along with confusion of not knowing what was going on was getting to him. He asked like he was waiting on his mother to speak back. He was happy that no one was around him, Sonny turned into that child that just needed his mother. The mother who was taken away from him too early, the mother that he never knew. Sonny needed Amoi more than his next breath, he was hurting knowing that this was the closest he would ever get to her. Placing his hand on her headstone, Sonny let silent tears fall from his eyes.

***

"Oh my god." Troi covered her mouth with her hands as tears slipped down her face. The scene before her made her sick. This wasn't the Sonny she knew, Troi knew Sonny was a bad boy but to witness it was something new. Pulling out her phone, she went to his contact and stared at it. Did she want to call him or give him the peace he wanted. She placed her phone down for a few seconds wondering if he'd be mad she'd followed him. She watched as Sonny broke down. The sight pulled at her heartstrings. Sonny didn't cry like this, this moment was something he needed. Troi was confused, she didn't know if she should go out there and be with him or start her car up and go home. "Fuck it." She said a silent prayer then climbed out of the car walking over to her man.

Hearing someone coming up behind him, Sonny snatched his gun from his waistline, and aimed. His finger only inches away from the trigger ready to lay a body down. He had to make it home to Troi by all means necessary. But when he saw her with her hands up over her head like she was surrendering, Troi stopped walking towards him to give him time to realize that it was her.

Her hands were shaking because she was scared, Troi hoped like hell she made the right decision on coming down here. Heart racing a hundred miles per minute because she didn't know what was about to happen. Sonny had every reason to be pissed with her but she wanted to help him. She knew Sonny needed her, Sonny just had to know this too.

When he dropped his gun back down to his waist, she felt relief. He wiped his tears because Troi had seen him weak one too many times. He didn't want her to label him as being weak when he was supposed to be her protector.

"Sonny, it's me baby." Troi walked towards him and wrapped her hands around him, while staring at the name on the headstone. *This is his mother, Amoi Nicole Vado.* Being wrapped in Troi arms was what Sonny needed right now, he needed his woman. For once Troi could feel the void his mother had left behind. For so long she'd filled it but while they sat at the cemetery she couldn't because his mother's spirit was present. She was covering her baby.

"What you doing here ma?" He finally asked slipping out of her embrace. He could feel her shaking with fear but still she was trying to comfort him. "You know ma, I hope I can love you the way my father didn't love my mama. From the stories I heard about him, he treated my mama like shit. The multiple women, the lies, and the drugs." The things Rich had told him made him hate his father. His mother didn't deserve half of what he did to her. He'd always wondered what happened to her but there was no straight story. Finding Alejandro there had to be fate. He noticed the fresh flowers on the ground and the dead ones in his hand. Like he was familiar. Like he knew Amoi more than Sonny ever would.

"She was beautiful Sonny." Troi stared at Amoi's picture on her headstone and Sonny looked just like her. "Baby, who,who is this." Troi pointed to Alejandro. With the way his emotions were running, Sonny forgot all about the dead body that was sitting beside him.

"A fucking DeLeon." Sonny's eyes turned back cold as he picked up the knife he used to slit Alejandro's throat.

"Baby, baby. Come back to me." Troi kneeled in front of Sonny and put her hands on his face. "Come back baby." Staring in her eyes, Sonny calmed down a little but he was still pissed off.

"What the fuck is he doing here?" Sonny kicked Alejandro's dead body.

"I'm not sure what he was doing here Sonny. We can't leave him out here though." Troi didn't know anything about the DeLeon family. The sight of him laying lifeless made Troi want to gag. Instead she kept her eyes locked in on Sonny's. He gave her a weak smile and pulled her into a hug. He kissed her on top of her head. Like she was heaven sent. Truly an angel that was trying to guide the devil.

This woman, whew, this woman was everything that Sonny needed. "I'll clean up here, you get rid of the body Sonny."

"Get rid of the body huh, What you know about that." Sonny stared at Troi in amazement. The thought of her holding him down at a time where shit was real made his dick hard.

"Go Sonny, Now." Her wish was his command. He picked Alejandro deadweight up, placing him in the trunk of his car and headed to one of his warehouses.

Running to her car Troi searched for anything that could help her get the blood off the tombstone. She found a rag in her trunk and the case of water she kept inside was enough for now. She grabbed the items then rushed back towards the tombstone and began pouring water over it while wiping it down with the rag. Troi was relieved most of the blood had been on the tombstone because she wasn't sure how she was going to get the blood off the grass.

Once the rag was worn out, Troi took off her cardigan, using it to clean the tombstone. She needed it spotless, to look like nothing happened.

After multiple trips from her car to the tombstone, it was finally clean and all she had to worry about was the grass.

"Think Troi, think." Almost in a panic she started pacing back and forth. *How am I gonna get this blood off the grass?* She pulled her phone out and called Sonny.

"Please pick up, please pick up." She whispered to herself. It was late, and dark and she was ready to get the fuck out of the cenetery. The shit that women did for the men they loved.

"What's up ma." Sonny was in the middle of getting rid of body parts and making sure Alejandro was never found again.

"I have everything done but the grass." Troi tried to talk in code, she wasn't used to this life but she knew enough about it, and watched enough movies to know she had to be vague.

"Alright ma, go home. I'll handle the rest. I have some shit that can help us with the grass. Troi?"

"Yes."

"I love you ma." Troi smiled from ear to ear. Despite everything that happened today, hearing him say that made this day a little better.

"I love you too Carson. Be safe."

"Always. You know I'm coming home to you." Sonny needed to hear them words from Troi today. This was all new to him but the way his cold heart fluttered when she said it, he knew Troi

was his one.

Chapter 20

Chicken quesadillas, tortilla and shrimp queso, and a rootbeer float was all Genie's baby had been craving lately. She'd had her abuelita whip her up her favorite dishes. As she dipped her quesadilla into the bowl of sour cream her baby kicked making her laugh. "Calm down baby," she spoke to her unborn while rubbing her belly and taking a bite of her food. "Mmm," she moaned in delight as her eyes closed while she savored the taste.

Gunz stormed into the dining room with his brows arched together in concern and Genie took notice.

"Why do you look like that?" She asked him while dipping a tortilla into her queso.

"Papi didn't come home last night." The news made Genie's brows knit together as well. That wasn't like their father and instantly her adrenaline began rushing. She'd last seen him after she told her white lie. She knew her father would handle Nitro but the thought of him being handled made Genie lose her appetite.

"You gonna tell me what made him have me shoot at Vado family after four months?" Gunz looked at her belly. The stomach she once hid was now protruding through the Milano Di Rouge t-shirt. Gunz hadn't questioned his fathers request and now he wished

he did. Because he could see the guilt all over his little sister's face.

Like she'd been caught and he'd caught her bluff. His intense stare

caused Genie to lower her eyes to her food. "You gotta tell me

something G. Papi called shots for you and now he's not answering

his phone, and ain't come home. That's not like him. So tell me

wassup," The tone of Gunz's voice was impatient. Like he knew his

sister had something she needed to get off her chest and was

exercising as much patience as he could.

"I told him Nitro raped me," Genie said a little above a

whisper and Gunz's head snapped as his eyes widened. He looked at

her like she was a demon while squinting his eyes to make sure he

was seeing things right. Shit, he felt the need to clean his ear to make

sure that he'd heard her correctly. The guilt on Genie's face revealed

the lie.

Gunz didn't know at what point his hand wrapped around

Genie's neck, but the scratching she did on his hand did little to stop

him. "Gideon!!" Selena's voice snapped him from his daze. The fear

in her voice caused him to let go of his sister. Genie's face was bright red, and she used both her hands to caress her neck as she coughed trying to catch her breath.

"You don't fucking lie about shit like that G! That shit is enough to put niggas entire family in the dirt! You fucking started some shit with a lie! A fucking lie G? I can't believe you. I'm a man, you don't lie about shit like that! That shit ain't cool!" Gunz raved and yelled in his sisters face angrily. He couldn't control his tone of voice nor the spit that flew from his mouth with each word.

Selena stared at the sibling rivalry confused. Gunz was on ten while Genie looked like she wanted to fall into a hole and hide. She was confused, and she wanted answers. "Genesis, what did you lie about?"

Gunz 'thoughts enraged him because he couldn't believe Genie had stooped so low. She'd done the unthinkable and he was disgusted. Ashamed even to be related to her.

"She told Papi that one of the Vado boys raped her. She was fucking that nigga the whole time!" Gunz answered for Genie. He was furious. He'd taken a shot at the Vado family after his father had told him. He hadn't asked any questions, or hesitated. He had shot until he saw Nitro on the ground and now a slight remorse filled him.

The war had been put to a stop and started back up over Genie. Selena's mouth opened slightly in shock as she looked at Genie to say something but in that moment. If all else failed Genie would cry crocodile tears.

"Genesis, dime que no es verdad" (Genesis, tell me it's not true) Selena took a seat at the table waiting for Genie to answer. Worry filled her face as Genie's tears gave her all the answers she needed. Her tears of guilt disgusted Gunz. She didn't even stay ten toes. Genie was panicking because she knew she fucked up. And Gunz wouldn't excuse her behavior.

"Tia, she did that shit, and if something happened to Papi imma ki" Selena put her finger up, halting the next word that would come out of Gunz's mouth. They didn't call him Gunz for no reason. He was lethal with the shit and he didn't make threats. He was more of a promise kind of guy.

"Gideon, you go cool off so I can talk to Genesis. Rafi and the rest of the guys are about to go looking for Alejandro. Go with them." She instructed. Selena's heart was heavy and she was trying to hold her family together. But her gut never lied. She'd felt it when her son was killed and she felt it now but still. She had hope, she was just a person that needed to see the carfax. Without proof she'd always have hope.

Gunz wanted to break the news to his auntie. The search was of no use. This move had been off script and when it came to family Alejandro was never off. He followed the same routine making sure his household was intact. He'd taken L's before and he didn't trip about it. Instead he was more careful.

As Gunz began to backpedal out of the dining room his cousin Rafi walked in with a worried look.

"We found this outside the gate." He told them while sitting a small package down on the table. Genie felt relief that someone was prolonging the conversation that Selena wanted to have. She was grateful for any interruption in hopes that she could think of a response for Selena's every question.

Gunz walked over to the package opening it. The tears that cascaded his face confirmed his biggest fear. His father was gone. The tattooed arm that read *DeLeon* was the proof Selena needed. She stood from her seat and walked over to the box peeking inside and the sight made her hand cover her mouth in fear. "No Alejandro," she denied. She wasn't accepting his death. Not even with the proof.

Her big brother had been her everything and to receive a message like this made it clear Genie had crossed a line that had been blocked off. She'd started a war that she'd ended and there was no telling how it would end this time because it was just beginning.

***

"Baby you have to wake up, do it for me please." Imani sat at Nitro bedside and cried, she cried for Nitro, cried for herself, but most importantly she cried for the baby she was carrying. The baby that her and Nitro made out of love, the baby that she prayed for. There was a pain in her chest that she wanted to get rid of. A pain that would stay until Nitro woke his ass up. It had been two weeks since Nitro was shot and Imani hadn't left his side yet. She didn't feel right with leaving him alone. When he woke up, she wanted her face to be the first face he saw.

"How's him holding up." Llanzo entered the room and touched Nitro's face. His nephew wasn't supposed to be laid out on a bed like this. Body filled with holes that had to be sewn up.

"He hasn't made any improvement yet. I'm so ready for him to wake up." Imani sighted laid her head on Nitro's stomach. She wipes her tears not wanting to share the intimate parts of herself with anyone except Nitro. She didn't want to appear to be weak.

Llanzo walked over to her and patted her back trying to console her. He wasn't used to having to do this, he didn't have a soft bone in his body, but Imani's cries were driving him off a wall making him try to be there for her. "You know mi neffew a soldier right, him going to make it out of this." Llanzo reassured her. He was more unsure than he was sure that Nitro would make it. He just had to say something that instilled hope while making Imani calm down. Although she continuously wiped tears away they came down like a rainstorm. Imani was hyperventilating from trying to hold her tears in and snot ran down her face.
The love Imani had for his nephew was visible.

"But it hurts to see him laying in this bed. He's not moving, he's not talking or cracking jokes. He's not doing anything. I'm not used to this. He needs to wake up, not for him, or for me." Llanzo stopped patting her back and looked at her strange. Imani was speaking in code and Llanzo was looking for clarity. "I'm pregnant." The room silent enough to hear a pin drop.

"Pregnant?" Llanzo couldn't hide his excitement, this is what he wanted for his nephews. He wanted them to have children that would carry on their family legacy for years to come. Every nigga in the game needed a down ass bitch beside him. Imani loved his nephew and as long as she loved him and had his child she would be right by his side.

He pulled Imani up from her chair, giving her a hug. Now that he knew she was pregnant he had to keep an eye on her. "Congratulations. mih know Denetro is going tuh be so happy wen him wake up. Yuh giving him a reason tuh live Imani. Tis life growing inside of yuh is wats going tuh wake Nitro up, there's no way in hell that him is leaving him family."

"I know, I just wish there was something I could do to make him wake up sooner, I miss hearing him. The more I hear silence the crazier I feel."

"Him will." Llanzo gave her another pat on the back and walked out the room to give her some privacy.

Sitting behind his desk, Llanzo leaned in his chair. Frustrated was the only way he was feeling right now. He wanted, no he needed for Nitro to wake up. He'd lost his brother and losing his kid would make him a failure. His phone rang cutting his thoughts in half. He stared at it for seconds before he answered.

"Speak tuh mih." Even though the number wasn't saved he recognized it.

"Llanzo I'm done. This feud, this war this beef between our families, I'm done with it! You have my word. You won." Selena was on the phone sounding almost distraught, she sounded like she was about to go crazy.

"What tis about Selena?" Llanzo questioned her. Not one to just agree with something someone else says,

"I just want a truce Llanzo, I'm tired of the blood shed between our families. It's been going on for too long now. You tell your boys to lay low and we'll tell ours to lay low. No more bloodshed Llanzo please." At this point it was almost as if she was begging. Selena's fear was evident. She was scared for the rest of her family lives. Selena didn't want to bury anyone else, she just wanted peace.

"Truce. As long as yuh boys stand down, mih nephews stand down." When he hung up the phone Llanzo couldn't help but wonder why the sudden change of heart when they had been the one who came back guns blazing. What made Selena want to call a truce and where the fuck was Alejandro? He pulled his phone out and called Selena back because he couldn't leave questions unanswered. It was unlike Alejandro to let Selena do the talking. If Selena was calling, it could only mean one thing, but he needed to hear it for himself.

Llanzo waited until Selena answered the phone. Without giving her a chance to fully speak Llanzo cut her off.

"Where's Alejandro?"

"He's gone, My brother is dead and I can't handle any more deaths. The DeLeons and Vado family beef has come to an end."

CLICK

Looking at the phone, Llanzo smiled because the Vados had won. They won the beef but his only question now was, which one of his nephews handled the job.

Chapter 21

Knock knock

Kill peeled his eyes off his TV and walked over to his door swinging it open. He didn't do unexpected visits. Especially not after the war with the DeLeon's and Kaylin running off with his product. He'd come to the conclusion that no one could be trusted. He swung the door open

pulling his gun out aiming it at the person at the other end.

"Give me one reason why I shouldn't blow yo fucking head off." Kill was enraged all over again. The audacity of this bitch to come to his house after the bullshit she did.

"Get the fucking gun out my face." Kaylin slapped the gun down and bypassed him into his home. He had every right to be mad at her but being greeted with a gun was the most disrespectful thing he ever did to her. "Have you lost yo fucking mind Kill." Kaylin pointed her finger in his face enraged. She stood toe to toe with Kill with a mug on her face. *His big ass is not about to intimidate me.* Kaylin thought to herself standing her ground. She rolled her eyes as he lowered his gun and went to take a seat. Getting comfortable as if they'd seen one another the night before. Like it hadn't been over a week. Kill looked at her like she was crazy.

"Kaylin, what the fuck is you doing in my house. What the fuck is stopping me from putting a bullet in your head?"

"Enough is a fucking nough." Kaylin snapped tired of the threats. She had come on a peaceful note but if Akiel wanted to choose violence. She would match his. She smoothly pulled her .380 out her purse and aimed at Kill. Best friends turned into enemies, going to war with one another. Both of them wore scowls on their faces. Who would have thought this would be the life Kill and Kaylin would be living. Kaylin was fed up with coming second to another woman. There was something about her woman's intuition that caused Kaylin to lose her mind when it came to Kill and Cher. "What's stopping me from putting a bullet in yo ass Kill?"

"If you pull it out you betta use it ma." Kill was impressed, this wasn't the Kaylin he met in high school. It wasn't even the same woman that he'd left with all his weed. Something was different about her. She was strapped, and prepared. The sight of her pulling a gun on him pissed him off and turned him on at the same time.

"Why am I not good enough for you, Kill? We been fucking with each other since high school. I know you. I study you, I know what you look like on a day to day basis. I know when you're sick, when somethings bothering you, when you're hungry, hell, I know everything about you. But I don't know the part of you that runs when that bitch tells you to. I can't recognize you around her. My feelings matter too, I always put you first and yet I come last to her. What does she have that I don't have? You go running to her and you walk to me. Are you fucking her?" Kaylin was furious, she needed answers and Kill was about to give them to her.

Kill lowered his gun and his eyes softened. Kaylin was a woman scorned and he'd been the one to scorn her.

"Why does she always come before me? You up and left me when she called, you ran without a second thought." Kill stepped towards Kaylin taking the gun out of her hand and hugged her.

"I'm sorry you feel this way ma, we've been rocking since high school. You're my rock, my ride or die and ain't no one coming before you and I mean that. This shit too organic for you to be feeling that way." Kill rubbed her back to soothe her. "You brave as fuck though, why you come back after stealing my shit." Kill broke the small silence between them.

"Yo shit at my house, I'm never dumb enough to steal and get rid of yo shit. That's not all though. I'm pregnant." Kill's world stopped when he heard the words. He hadn't been prepared to hear them. He was careful most of the time and he really couldn't remember when he slipped up.

"You're pregnant?" He asked making sure that she was sure. He was unprepared and news like this was enough to change a nigga's entire life around. He needed Kaylin to be sure.

"That's what I said, Akiel." She pulled her positive pregnancy test out, passing it to him.

"Are you keeping it?" He asked, wondering if this was how him and Kaylin would finally be together. It was unexpected, and unwanted but ultimately it was Kaylins choice. He couldn't dictate what she did with her body, but his question should have told her enough. His reaction was still and hers wasn't. The steam in her ears was evident.

"Yes, I'm keeping *our* baby." Kill didn't know how to feel, he wanted to be happy but the fear inside of him of being a father was real. Kids slowed you down and Kill was at the point of his life where he couldn't be slowed down. A child would be his weakness and he would kill the whole fucking city if something or somebody messed with his offspring. He didn't need that right now. "Are you mad?" Kaylin was filled with joy when she found out she was pregnant now that joy was descending seeing the look on Kill face.

"We'll figure it out, we always do." Kill pulled Kaylin into a hug wanting to hide his disdain. it was disrespectful and he was aware of it. His world was about to do an entire 360 and he honestly didn't know how to feel.

***

A bright light was always the sign of life after death. The light wasn't bright like the sun, but more so like the light that a doctor held into your eyes. But except there was no doctor holding Nitro's eyelids open. In fact, the image of the little boy at the end of the light made Nitro keep his eyes shut. Somehow he felt a connection. One that made him run towards the young boy with dreads who cried because he looked lost. Nitro saw the resemblance and at first he couldn't remember from where. But as he got closer and closer to the young boy he realized that he was a spitting image *of him. **That's my son?** He thought to himself while running full speed towards the young boy. His arms were wide open inviting Nitro into them. And the closer Nitro got the more out of breath he felt. Like he was leading himself into death. But what parent wouldn't die for their kid?*

Imani's sniffled tears as she laid beside Nitro. The cramping in her stomach had been the worst she'd ever experienced. It wasn't period cramps, and she knew it. She knew exactly where the pain was coming from and she was unable to do anything about it except take it. Taking the pain caused her heart to ache. The positive pregnancy test she'd seen yesterday was slowly turning negative. Her body and her baby weren't cooperating with one another and she could feel it. A part of Imani wanted to go to a doctor but it was of no use. She was early, heavy bleeding only meant one thing and she didn't need a doctor to tell her that. Instead she laid beside her man. As a machine pumped life into him. For the past four weeks she'd stayed by his side praying, asking god to cover him and give him a chance to be there for her and his child. Even if he'd gone half on a baby with the devil, every child needed their parents.

But today the grief was heavy, she was mourning her baby, *their baby.* By herself and it was driving her up a wall. She was losing hope. Feeling like maybe Nitro could leave her so he could guide their baby. Only if she had known that he wanted the same thing.

The feeling of his hand squeezing her thigh caused Imani's eyes to widen. For a second she thought she was becoming delusional until he squeezed a second time. She quickly sat up and pressed the button for the on call doctor that Llanzo had paid to keep Nitro alive. Even if it were minimally. At first Imani couldn't understand why, and now she did.

"Nitro baby, I'm right here. I'm not leaving you." She whispered to him as she watched his eyelids flutter open then closed. He was heavily sedated. He wanted to be up but his eyelids were so damn heavy they kept closing on their own.

"Get up off di bed," Dr. Paul instructed and Imani wasted no time complying. She watched as the Jamaican doctor went to work on him. Removing the tube from his mouth. She wringed her fingers together nervously. Imani hadn't realized how Nitro waking up had made her push her pain to the side. Making it subside a little bit.

"Blink twice if you can feel dis," the doctor instructed as he ran a pen across Nitro's feet. When he blinked twice Imani closed her eyes. *Thank you God for watching over him.* Imani's tears of sorrows flipped to tears of joy like a switch as she watched Nitro with both eyes open blinking as the doctor tested all his nerves. He'd been shot four times and Imani's hope had been built on delusion. She had known niggas who died after being shot once. She'd prayed and prayed and a part of her didn't believe her prayer would be accepted but it was and she was grateful.

She sat in the chair beside him staring intensely at the doctor going to work. She just wanted to make sure he was good.

Nitro turned his eyes from the doctor to Imani. He stared at her not saying a word because his throat was so dry from the lack of speech. But he noticed her. *She been here the whole time. She different now.* He wondered if his near death experience had changed her. He saw her tears of joy but he also saw her tears of hurt. They were the same tears his son had before he had to go. He lifted a weak hand and placed it onto hers as the doctor turned him over onto his side. Nitro squeezed her hand for reassurance. He was alive.

"You are a very lucky mon, yuh Vado's ave tough skin. Men ave died fi less, and women have left men fi less." Dr. Paul spoke to him as he finished his exam. He gave Imani a respectable smile. She'd been beside Nitro for a month and hadn't moved much. She was the most solid American woman he'd seen. Imani had hopped on a jet with Nitro staying by his side every step of the way. She put him first and it was rare to come by that. Even in Jamaica.

As soon as Dr. Paul exited the room Imani climbed back into the bed and laid beside Nitro. He pulled her onto him, worsening his pain but it didn't matter. He could see that Imani needed him. Dr. Paul's words held weight. He was their family doctor. Anytime they got sick when they came to Jamaica he was there. Imani was heaven sent and Nitro just knew that he needed to get back to her. He'd been so close to death, but leaving her behind hadn't been an option. *God got little man.* He thought about his son.

Chapter 22

"I ain't been home in a minute," Sonny shared as he stared out the window of the private jet. He and his brothers were taking a trip to Jamaica per Llanzo's request. A trip to Jamaica only met one thing. It was time to talk business. Being in the clouds physically and mentally gave him a sense of peace. So much had been going on lately and after handling Alejandro and getting news that Nitro was up, Sonny's energy had been restored. For once in a long time he felt peace. He and Troi were on good terms, his conscience felt vindicated, and Nitro was up. The foreign feeling made him slightly uneasy but he welcomed it. *Peace is good, he* reminded himself of Troi's words. The thought of his babygirl caused him to look at his phone.

"Baby bro sprung than a mufucka. Tighten up." Kill joked as he passed a glass of Henny to his younger brother. Sonny was anxious, like he was ready to get back home to Troi. Kill was thankful for the appearance that Troi had made into Sonny's life. Who would've known the cure to their brother was the bartender at their business. It slightly surprised Kill that Troi had tamed him. He owed her. She'd been able to do something none of them had been able to do.

"Hennessy will undo all this shit." Sonny warned as he held restraint placing the glass onto the table. Rich and Kill both stared at him in shock.

"Baby bwoy is growing up," Rich joked giving Sonny a raised brow. Sonny internally winced at the *baby boy* term, but on the outside he held his composure and his nose slightly flared. He rose from his seat and walked over to the minibar and poured himself a cup of Dussè.

"What? Y'all thought I was gon stay like that forever? I fucked up with the whole DeLeon shit. That shit eat at me everyday. I'm just trying to be better." Sonny confessed.

Rich scoffed while shaking his head. "At di expense of Chasity. " Rich reminded him. Keeping his daughter's name alive. Sonny would have to live with her death being on his conscience. If they were going to speak on his fuck ups. They would speak on the biggest one. Rich would make sure of it. He'd noticed Sonny avoiding him. *Being better.* Sonny had changed and Rich still couldn't be proud of him. Because he'd changed too late.

Sonny felt the blow and he downed the drink and retreated to the back of the jet. Once again he was avoiding the confrontation with his older brother knowing that it could get ugly because of their temper. But he was in no position to have a temper. He'd acknowledged his fuck up and the cost it had been. But he was trying and it was clear that Rich didn't give a fuck about a healed Sonny.

Kill shook his head from side to side downing his shot of Hennessy. He thought of his words wisely not trying to seem insensitive. "The guilt already eating at him bro, you gon push him over the edge?" Kill asked, wanting to know if Rich would purposely cause their younger brother to go down a path of destruction. They'd already lost too much and almost lost one of their brothers.

"Mi don't giv a fuck. Mi lose mi dawta behind dat nigga careless actions. If he's changed him haffi accept that shit."

Sonny heard the words clear as day and he just returned his stare back out the window. To the clouds.

Thirty minutes later they were greeted by their uncle with a wide smile on his face. Like he was proud and had great news to share with them. He passed the three of them pre rolled blunts as he individually hugged each of them.

"Mi wan fi chat tuh yuh," Llanzo told them while leading them into his office. He took a seat behind his desk and the brothers made their way over to the couch across from him.

"Mi don tink mi eva seen you skin yuh teeth that wide," Sonny told his uncle as he lit his blunt. Seeing his Uncle Llanzo in a good mood put him in one.

"One of yuh give mi a reason tuh skin yuh teeth dis wide," Llanzo nodded to his youngest nephew. The one who had gotten them in this world wind. "Which one of yuh kill Alejandro DeLeon," the surprised looks on Rich and Kill's face cause Llanzo to sit back. His eyes went from Rich, to Kill, to Sonny who sat there nervously. Like he'd been caught committing another crime that could possibly add onto their family war. Llanzo locked eyes with Sonny keeping his eyes trained on him as he spoke.

"Badrick did yuh kill him?" Rich placed his eyes onto his uncle realizing that he hadn't even given him the decency to give him eye contact. Rich's heart raced for the first time in a long time he felt himself conforming to a child that was bouncing around with the idea on whether they should lie. Rich knew what was at stake and he hadn't done the job. Which meant the one thing he wanted in the world he wouldn't have. His family's empire was down to his two younger brothers.

"Get out," his uncle ordered. Disappointment laced in his tone.

"Akiel, did you kill Alejandro?"

Kill sat in complete shock as he realized his little brother had saved the day. He chuckled while shaking his head from side to side looking at Sonny too. The look on his face was proud. Like he'd just watched his brother take his first steps. Sonny had solved his own problem which solved all their problems.

Llanzo could feel the excitement radiating off Kill that he didn't dare ask him to step out. Instead he continued.

"Carson, did you kill Alejandro DeLeon?"

"Yea Unc," Sonny owned it, no hesitation. Llanzo stood from his seat and opened his arms wide as he waved Sonny over to him. All the anxiousness Sonny had felt went out the window. He finally felt accepted like he'd done something right. Like he'd righted his wrongs. He stood up and embraced Llanzo, who squeezed him patting him on the back.

"Dey don wan no more smoke" Llanzo told his nephews and Kill let out a breath of relief. It finally felt like shit was over. It had taken Sonny to man up to finish the job and he couldn't help but hug his brother. His change was evident.

"You did good lil bro," Kill reassured him in his ear as he embraced him in a hug. Sonny nodded towards him and shrugged his shoulders cockily.

"Troi making a man out of a nigga. Imma wife her bro" Sonny confessed in Kill's ear. He couldn't take all the credit for his changed ways. Troi had come in and made him want to change for her. For once everyone was proud of him but she was to thank for that. She'd rearranged his sights and had him on a straight line. Drinking less, taking meds, cleaning up bodies. Troi had proven to be heaven sent and Sonny wanted to make sure everyone knew she was it. She was to thank for his change in behavior.

"Say no more bro." Kill pulled back placing his hands up. Sonny was a grown man, making grown man decisions and as long as they were good ones Kill would always have his back. The idea of

Troi being a permanent fixture in their life and Sonny being permanently like this enlightened Kill.

He stepped out of the office leaving Llanzo and Sonny to talk. In a game of business Sonny had won unknowingly and while one brother was proud of him the other twinged with jealousy.

Kill walked out the doors. "He accepted what he did, and fixed that shit. Let him breath." He told Rich seriously.

Sonny took his seat across from his uncle wondering what was next. And Llanzo wasted no time telling him. "Di family bizniz being pass dung tuh yuh." Llanzo told him as he poured the both of them a glass of vodka. Sonny's eyes widened in shock. And Llanzo chuckled. "Mi tell yuh brothas whoeva get to Alejandro first wud tek ova."

Sonny's jaw slightly dropped but it caught it before it could hit the floor. He hadn't known what was on the line and inside of him there were fireworks going off. The one thing he'd dreamed about having he was getting and he was like a kid in a candy store on the inside. "How did yuh do it?" Llanzo asked as he passed Sonny the glass. The question caused Sonny to have a few of his own. And once he answered his uncle he would get them.

"Mi go tuh mommy's grave and him there. Bringing har new flowers. Wah dat about?"

Llanzo sat his drink on the table as Sonny's words resonated through him. *She did really fucking wid that nigga.* The confirmation from Sonny had slightly shocked him. Years ago his brother had come to home to the accusations and Llanzo had brushed it off. Mistaking her for a good girl, and a great wife but Amoi's betrayal had been revealed at a graveyard.

"Yuh dad tink Amoi di fucking wid Alejandro. Him kill har in di DeLeon home and Alejandro kill him." Llanzo put the pieces together. DaJuan had left him with his suspicions years ago, but Sonny's victory confirmed it. The news to Sonny offended him slightly and Llanzo watched to see the difference in his nephews act when he was triggered. When Sonny didn't move an inch and instead his nose slightly flared Llanzo didn't hesitate to continue.

"Mi have fi train yuh pan how tuh run di farm and distribute product. Di next load in a month. Mi will be sending fi yuh den. Till den, chill out." Llanzo told him changing the subject. He filled his glass again and put it up to Sonny's.

"Tuh new beginnings neffew," He put his glass in the air. Sonny tapped his against his uncle, nodding his head.

"To new beginnings," he toasted and down his drink. The day was starting off on the right foot. Life was looking up for him and he couldn't complain. He was on the cloud and he couldn't wait to share his news with his brothers. Especially Nitro.

***

"My muthfucking nigga." Sonny slapped hands with Nitro as soon as he walked into the room his brothers were in. His fucking ace was woke and he was happier than a muthafucka.

"This nigga Sonny pulling up being loud and shit." Nitro chuckled. He was almost back to himself, at least that what he tried telling himself. The bullets had taken him to death and back but he was still standing.

"How dem bullets feel mih boy. How yuh doing." Rich placed his hand on Nitro's shoulder. The news of his little brother getting shot almost broke him. The last thing he needed was to lose Nitro. Rich honestly couldn't stand the news of losing anyone else who shared his blood. He glanced at Sonny wondering how he'd done the impossible. Jealousy coursed through his body along with anger. But he quickly tried to erase the thoughts out of his mind.

"I'm doing as good as a nigga who got shot can do." Sitting up in his bed Nitro grabbed the water that was at his bedside and took a sip. His throat was dry since they took the tube out.

"I'm happy you woke bro, we missed you." Kill slapped hands with Nitro as he took a seat beside him on the bed. With all the shit that Kill had on his plate, with Kaylin his mind was everywhere. He wanted to tell his brothers and see what they had to say but right now it was all about chillin with the bros. He could hold his shit in a little longer.

"Nigga I'm happy you came in here with some sense unlike these fools. Y'all need to take notes. This how you approach a nigga that been shot." All of them laughed together. It was a minute since the brothers were all together. It took Nitro getting shot for them to get together. It honestly felt good to be in the presence of each other.

"So, I got some shit I need to say." Sonny was ecstatic about everything that was about to happen. He was finally leveling up. He was in love with a bad bitch and he was about to take over the family business.

"Wassup man." Rich was first to rude him. He dying to hear what Sonny had to say, even though he already knew what the fuck was coming.

"I killed Alejandro." Kill and Rich knew, he looked over to Nitro to make sure he heard him.

"Get the fuck out of here." Nitro went into a coughing fit, that news literally took his breath away. Kill grabbed his cup of water off the nightstand and put his straw up to Nitro's lips so he could catch his breath.

"I didn't mean to almost kill you bro." Sonny smirked. He waited on Nitro to regain his composure before he continued. "As I was saying before this nigga tried to die on us again. I killed Alejandro and Uncle Llanzo offered me the head of the farm. He stepping down and want me to step all the way up."

"Congrats man." Nitro and Kill was happy for their little brother, if anybody deserved this job it was Sonny. This nigga did what no one else had the balls to do.

"Wat did yuh tell him? Did yuh take di job." Rich asked as his dark skin turned pale. No congrats, no smile, nothing, the look on Rich face revealed his envy and Kill and Nitro peeped. They were unsure if Sonny noticed it and instead of pressing on it they both placed a mental note to speak to Rich about it.

"What you mean man, of course I took it, this what I've been waiting for." Sonny didn't realize that Rich's envy was envy instead of hate. The hate he'd spewed to Sonny for so long seemed normal, to a point where his envy and hate were both identical. Sonny was blind to the vibe his brother was putting out. Rich disapproved of Sonny being his boss. The position was supposed to be his. Sonny had years to go before the throne was rightfully passed down to him but he'd bypassed it all.

"How yuh gone run a business bowy, yuh still have breast milk on yo breath." Rich cracked a smile, he tried to not show his jealousy for Sonny but it was all on his face. Rich was pissing Kill off. Rich was probing at Sonny. Trying to see how far he could go and Kill couldn't understand why. Sonny being on a better path was a good thing. Rich had taken an L and Kill respected it. But he was just taking it too far. Rich was trying to give Llanzo a reason to tell Sonny he was incapable but Kill wouldn't allow it.

"Congrats bro. You're gon, make a dope ass boss, you the king man. Rich let me holla at you real quick." Kill told his older brother as he stepped out of the room and onto the balcony that wrapped around the house. Rich followed him seething with anger.

"What the fuck is yo problem man." Kill wasted no time, he needed to know what was going on with Rich.

"Kill, mih a yuh both know how hard mih work for tis job. Mih little brutha is mih boss. That don't sit well wit mih. Sonny is a hothead, him can't handle it." Rich's voice went up with every word he said. Just talking about Sonny's victory pissed him off.

"What if he can handle it Rich, Sonny's not the same little boy that we raised. He's a grown ass man that can make his own moves. You need to give him more respect than you do. I know you used to playing his daddy but you his brother."

"Respect? Did yuh forget dat di reason all tis shit start did cuz of sonny. Sonny di reason dat wi even in this bullshit. Mi dawta lose her life cause a nigga waste liqua on him fucking shoes kill. Dat di type of nigga yuh wa running the family business, yuh wa a hotheaded nigga like dis." Rich leaned over the balcony and looked at the water that was in the pool beneath them. It felt good to finally get that out. He'd been holding it in and now that it was out he felt like a weight had been lifted off his chest.

"There it goes, you blame our little fucking brother for Chasisity getting killed. Let's not forget the fact that when she was shot, it was Sonny who found Chas when she was gunned down. You was entertaining ya mistress. He fucked up, he always do. But he hasn't in a long time. You can blame him but gotta take some of the blame as well. If Missy wasn't in your face, your daughter would've been by your side. Nigga fuck up everyday B, but let's not start the blame game cause that shit is just unfair. Let lil bro be great" Rich turned around and stared at Kill, he was ready to strike but Kill wasn't who he was angry at.

Kill shook his head and reentered the mansion and went back to kick it with his brothers. Rich was the last of his problems right now. Nitro had finally woken up and Sonny was about to take the family business to a whole new level. Rich had to deal with his shit on his own.

Chapter 23

"Goodnight mommy baby." Cher kissed Enoch on his cheeks and watched him as he went to sleep. He reminded her so much of Chasity when she was still a baby. She was constantly comparing the two to keep her daughter spirit alive. She somehow remembered every single thing Chas did as a baby and Enoch was slowly turning out like his big sister. She watched him suck his thumb, and cuddle up with his bear and it brought tears to her eyes. It was around the holiday season and she was missing her oldest baby, something serious. Tears filled her eyes but she refused to let them fall. Instead when he fell all the way asleep she snuck out of his room and closed his door.

"Cher yo phone ringing." Wynni called from the living room. She rushed to her phone, and saw it was Kill so she answered it.

"Merry Christmas Akiel." Cher smile was brighter than the sun shining outside.

"Merry Christmas Cher. How you and the kids doing, we miss y'all down here." Taking a deep breath Cher took in the sound of Kill voice. She missed him more than she missed anyone else back home. If it was up to her Akeil would have been here with her and her babies.

"We're doing okay, they're starting to miss their dad though so I can't stay away for too much longer." Kill nodded his head in agreement even though Cher couldn't see him. Kill agreed with a lot of the stuff Cher did but taking the kids away from Rich for this long didn't sit well with him.

"How's my nephews?"

"They are good, growing before my eyes. I feel like I've been grieving so much that the time is passing me by. I miss you." Cher's words came out as a small moan. She missed Kill so fucking much, he'd been her support and that shit held weight in her heart. He was doing more than her "husband" and a small part of her wished that he could take that role from his brother. Cher knew that was wishful thinking. It would never happen. Rich wouldn't allow it, and quite frankly in the back of her mind she knew Kill wouldn't either. He was just too solid like that. Loyal to his family no matter the circumstance.

She was married to his brother and even though that was soon to change, this wasn't the person that Cher was raised to be.

"Miss ya to ma. Check ya bank account in the morning, I sent you a Christmas gift." It was the little things that mattered to her. Kill made sure that her and her boys never needed for anything. Not that she was broke or anything, but the gesture of him doing that out the kindness of his heart made her hurt flutter.

"You know you don't have to do that right."

"I know I don't have to, but I do. I'm not gon hold you too long. Tell my nephews I love them and I betta see y'all at our family dinner."

Cher felt relief as the words left his lips. An invitation to one of their New Year family traditions. "Goodnight Akiel." After hanging up the phone Cher put it up to her chest where her heart was. It felt as if it was beating out her chest, this is what Akiel Vado did to her.

"Bitch spill, what the fuck is going on between you and Kill." Cher jumped at the sound of Wynni's voice. The entire time she was talking to Kill, she forgot that Wynni was right by her.

"Girl, what you talking about." Cher walked to the kitchen and grabbed her a bottle of wine and two wine glasses. "Wine?"

"Yeah, pour me some wine and tell me what the fuck is going on." Cher blew out a sigh of frustration knowing that her best friend wasn't about to let it go.

Getting comfortable on the couch, Cher looked over at Wynni and she felt the tears trickling in her eyes.

"There's nothing going on with me and Akiel. I do wish that I would have met Kill first though. He's everything that I wish Rich was." Cher dropped her head in shame, this was the first time that she had admitted this out loud. "Wynni, I think I'm in love with Akeil." The tears that were threatening to come out of her eyes finally fell.

"Awhhhh Cher, dont cry." Getting out her seat, Wynni went and put her arms around Cher and let her cry. Cher needed to get all of this out.

"I fe-feel so damn ba-ba-bad Wynni." Cher could barely get her sentences out. She was hurting and she was hurting bad. How in the hell could she be in love with her husband's brother.

"Please don't tell anyone." Cher asked as she finally calmed down.

"You know me better than that. You're playing with fire though Cher. Let that man go and focus on yo husband, even if you don't go back to your husband DO NOT GO TO HIS BROTHER."

"It's just wishful thinking, I would never do that to Rich. As much as I hate that man, I have to admit my love for him runs deeper than that. You think I could live with myself if I fucked with his brother?" Wynni looked at Cher and busted out laughing, the wine was getting to her, "What the fuck is so funny?" Cher couldn't help but to laugh with her, Wynni's head was laid back on the couch and she had tears coming out of her eyes from how hard she was laughing.

"I mean Cher, can you picture Rich's face right now if he found out you were messing with Kill. He would probably kill both of you. I can see it now, breaking news on the tv for everyone to see." Cher laughed because she pictured the look on Rich's face.

"That shit would be funny, but he would never know." Shrugging her shoulders, Cher set back and thought about her life. All the shit she had been through with Rich, was finally getting left behind her.

After putting on a movie for them to watch, Cher thought about the life she would have had with Kill. Thirty minutes later the TV was watching her because she was consumed with her own thoughts. *Cher and Kill. That doesn't sound too bad.* Were Cher's last thoughts before she drifted off to sleep while thinking of Akeil muthafucking Vado.

***

Pregnancy glow was a thing that Kaylin marveled in. Happiness radiated through her pores and the extra sparkle in her eye Kill noticed. The extra gloss had him hypnotized. The idea of becoming a family he'd been a little weary about. But the more excited Kaylin got, it added to his a little. Since Sonny was taking over the thought of leaving the game was on pause. He had to have his brothers back for his rise. Although this life wasn't for a baby Kill had thought up a solution and tonight he would present it to Kaylin.

It was date night. It had been a while since the two of them just had a minute to themselves. Plus Kill was trying to relieve some of Kay's anxiety around the friendship he and Cher had so he kept it limited. He checked up on her and the kids once a week just to make sure they were straight and didn't need anything. Kill didn't know where or how Cher had become a soft spot for him. Because of Kaylin and her insecurities he kept it respectful. Only calling Cher when Kaylin was out of earshot.

The thought of Kill and Cher ceasing communication gave Kay a peace of mind. "Where are we going?" She asked him as soon as she walked into the living room. The grey Milano Di Rouge shirt and black jean skirt went perfectly with her grey and black knee length fur Uggs. The mink coat and fox fur hat gave her a bad bitch look.

"Don't worry about it. As long as you comfortable that's all that matters. There's a car outside for us."

Kaylin's face wore a look of surprise. Kill had outdone himself. She was very just used to him being the driver and she being the passenger. But here he was taking it up a notch giving her butterflies. The kind that made her nervous. Akiel had stepped up and she wished it would be forever.

She followed him out the door and the all black tinted SUV greeted them in the front. The driver opened the door allowing her to enter, and when she did the yellow flower teddy bear on the seat made a wide smile appear on her face. "Thank you,"

"A nigga just getting started." Kill told her as he took a seat beside her. Kaylin's cheeks hurt from smiling so hard, she used her hands to pat them down causing Kill to chuckle. "This is what you wanted right? A nigga all in for you right? I'm doing my best to show you what a picture perfect day in our life could be like together. That shit ain't always guaranteed." He explained and Kaylin's eyes gleamed with tears of joy. He was trying for her. Friends to lovers unexpectedly and she was accepting it. She was accepting what he was offering.

"I knew you could do it, you always been this person. Only thing different now is the title on it. You okay with that?"

"If I wasn't okay, there wouldn't be a title ma."

Kaylin rolled her eyes up playfully and Kill used his fingers to gently turn her face towards his. "A title is the only thing that makes this shit between you and I different. You being a baby mama is ghetto and I couldn't let you go out like that. So I made you my girl, eventually my wife."

Kaylin's eyes widened slightly and suddenly it was like the high she'd been on had been blown. Kill was saying things he'd never said before and a part of her conscience ate at her. "Do you feel like I trapped you? Everything your saying sounds good but is it really what you want to do? You doing it cause of the baby and you don't have to Akiel." As soon as the words fell from Kaylin's lips an overwhelming feeling took over her. Tears welled in her eyes and a lone tear slipped from them.

Kill wiped the tear away with his thumb and picked her chin up off her chest. "Look at me ma," he trained his eyes on her and for some reason, Kaylin couldn't hold it together. The hormones had her all over the place and the fear of him taking her up on her offer and leaving made her sick to her stomach. "I always wanted this shit. The title shit. But the friendship came first and it meant too much to me to fuck it up Kay. So that's why there wasn't no titles. The bond we have is different Kay and you here to stay. A nigga putting all his faith in this, and I need you to too. Don't second guess this. Don't second guess me. I got you. Haven't I always?"

Kaylin's tears continued falling but her hormones had turned her tears of fear to tears of happiness. Akiel's words were music to her ear. He'd reassured her and hearing it from the horse's mouth was better than driving herself crazy mentally. She nodded her head and grabbed a piece of tissue out her purse dabbing her eyes. "Pregnancy turning Killa Kay soft," he joked lightening up the atmosphere. Kaylin giggled and nudged his arm.

"Wasn't saying that the other day."

Kill chuckled at her remark. He was happy she brought it up. It was better her than him. "I'm glad you said that." The car came to a complete halt and Kaylin stared out the window confused. The area looked abandoned, a few buildings surrounded them but nothing about the scenery screamed date.

"Where are we?" She asked as the driver opened the door letting her out.

"It's our first date baby. You got promoted to wifey so we doing wifey shit." He placed his hand on the small of her back. "I told you I'm trying Kay. When I say I'm trying. I mean trying to keep us all alive. You gotta know how to protect yourself ma. You see how shit goes down with my family. I need you and my pickney to be straight at all times." Kill explained as he led the way into one of the buildings. Kaylin heard his words and she took them all in. A small part of her filled with disappointment when she realized their first date was not your average first date. A table with different arsenal and ammo came into view. *A hood niggas first date is shooting.* She thought to herself. Why hadn't she known.

"I told you the only thing changed is the title and that shit comes with lessons." Kill passed her the protective glasses while handing her a handgun. "Follow me."

Kaylin was like a kid at school. Her eyes stayed focused on his hand as she moved her hand in sync with his. She hadn't even realized that he was showing her how to dismantle a gun until she saw his in different pieces on the table. When she looked down at her own in surprise Kill smirked and kissed her on her neck. Something about seeing Kay with a piece made his dick hard. Kaylin's hair on the back of her neck stood up as she shivered slightly. "What I gotta do to get more of that. Shit a little tongue action too." Kaylin responded. Kill lips on her had opened her sexual intentions for the night. She was horny and one kiss was enough to make her wanna say 'fuck this shit, it's time to fuck.' But she knew how important this was to Kill

"I can keep going as long as you can put it back together, without my help."

Kaylin looked from him to the table and shrugged her shoulders. "Okay," Kill lightly tapped her on her ass and pulled a chair up sitting behind her. He sat her into his lap and gave her a kiss like she was kiss to start.

Kaylin's hips slowly grinded onto Kill as he gave her kisses. He tilted her neck to the side giving himself a view of what she was doing as his tongue ran across her neck. "Mm mm" he warned her as she picked up one of the wrong pieces. Kaylin put it down and she felt the temperature in her body go up. Kill's lip on her body turned her on and she had a hard time concentrating, retracing the steps they had taken to take the gun apart.

Once she was at the last piece Kill sat her onto the table while remaining in his seat. He placed his hand under her skirt, rolling it up as he pulled down her G string. He nodded to the other gun on the table. "Put the other gun together so I could bless you for a job well done." He kissed her inner thigh the minute Kaylin grabbed the dismantled gun trying to use her first concentration technique. But when Kill kissed her pearl and used his tongue to separate her lips she almost lost it. *Fuck this.* She placed the gun down and seconds later Kill's head was up. She frowned and he gave her a head nod.

"A nigga doing too much for you? Cause this ain't up for debate."

Kaylin sucked her teeth and picked the gun up again. She was already hot and bothered and there was no way he could stop now. Her pussy had been ready to be led into euphoria before he'd ever gone down. She picked the pieces up and grinded her hips against his face. "Right fucking thereeeeee," she moaned as she threw her head back. Kill's tongue played with her clit like a bat to a ball. He slid two fingers in her wetness and Kaylin couldn't take it any more. She sat the gun down knowing there was no way she'd get anything done and held Kill's head in place.

He chuckled in between her thighs while still going to work. Kaylin's back bucked everytime and she wrapped her legs around his neck. Kill nibbled a bit and sucked her clit as he ran his tongue all around her. The kisses he placed to her lips made a shock go through Kay's body and she couldn't help but squeal. Her moans filled the ear and it was music to Kill's ears.

He loved Kaylin with everything in him. Always had. But the fear of a relationship fucking up their friendship always put him at bay. But they had taken the next step. God had placed them in the next step and Kill vowed to protect, and please her every step of the way. Loving her was easy. And as he sucked her soul from her pussy she gave him life. Her juices filled his mouth overflowing as it wet his goatee.

He gave her one last kiss on her lips and sat back full. Full of her. "This title shit sure does make everything feel ten times better." She told him as she tried catching her breath as she came down from her orgasmic high.

Kill nodded in agreeance and wrapped his hand around her neck as he stood up. "This title shit is forever. So I hope you know that Kay."

"I wouldn't have forever without you." She gave him a peck on his lips. The taste of her juices on his lips made her moan.

"Yo ass don't get enough and you a little hardheaded." He chuckled as he put the gun together in less than a minute. "It's time to get back to work ma."

Chapter 24

Three months, fifteen weeks to be exact. Cher's belly flopped nervously as she entered Footprints. It had been 105 days since she'd last seen Rich and a part of her had jitters. Not jitters of excitement but jitters of unknowing. She'd popped back up into town for their traditional New Years dinner and as much as she'd wanted to skip out on it she couldn't. This tradition was one that Chas had always requested and Cher owed her baby girl that. Her boys missed their dad and Cher could admit she missed being in Atlanta. The familiarity of it all. The family she'd married into had become her family. She couldn't not come back. Kill was here and as much as she didn't want to admit it, she wanted to see him.

"Welcome back," the sound of his voice made butterflies come and just as fast as they came so did the guilt. Cher spun on her heels and stood face to face with Kill. She pressed her lips tightly together to prevent drooling. Kill wore a knitted red Gucci turtleneck sweater, green and red Gucci's slacks with loafers. His locs were neatly retwisted and a gold chain hung from his neck, wrist was on freeze and his ears were blinding. Cher's womanhood trembled as she stared at the rare smile on his face.

"I'm back but I don't feel welcomed. Where is everyone?"

"They on they way. Everything gone be fine today. It's nothing but love and family. You straight. Where's my nephews?"

"Wynni is on her way with them. I thought I'd have to throw down in the kitchen." Cher told him as she entered the kitchen. The new head chef was at work and Cher eyed him like a hawk. Like she was a food critic and making sure that he made everything perfectly. There was no room for error. Dinner was in an hour and with all the tension that was bound to be in the room, the food needed to be the least of everyone's worries. "How has everything been? How's Sonny and Nitro?"

"Everything is everything. Sonny is finally growing up. Nitro is… adjusting" Kill tried finding the perfect set of words. Cher had a lot on her plate to be worried about other than Sonny and Nitro. Kill could tell she was nervous and trying to make conversation before she pulled her hair out.

"A lot of days I cry. Because I can't feel Chas where I'm at. But today I don't feel like crying. I feel like this is the closest I'll get to her again. Being at the very place she died, with the people she loved the most. Now I can feel her and it makes a part of me want to stay." Cher confessed. She was in a daze staring straight ahead at this point.

Kill pulled her in for a hug. "Well today there's no crying. We missed you. Everyone did. Even Rich." Kill whispered. Cher deeply inhaled the Tom Ford black cologne with her eyes closed. Being wrapped in his arms felt like therapy. And when his arms abruptly let her go, her eyes shot back open.

Kill slowly made his way away from Cher and beside Kaylin. The belly she sported and the mug on her face made Cher want to stomp her out. Anger, rage, jealousy, and every other negative emotion infiltrated Cher's mind.

Kill noticed the confusion while Kaylin noticed the envy. The little bit of anger that had consumed her from the vision of Cher and Kill had evaporated. Instead a smirk graced her face as she rubbed her belly. *This bitch is bothered.*

"What's good family!" Sonny's voice cut through the air slicing through the tension as he entered the kitchen. He raised his eyebrow in surprise as he noticed Cher in attendance. He smiled so wide his entire grill set showed blinding her.

"Carson!!" Cher squealed genuinely happy to see him. The relationship between the two was more platonic than the relationship Cher had with any other brothers. She'd been Sonny's only maternal figure and helped guide him through life until he spread his own wings.

Troi stood back stunned that Sonny shined a little brighter after seeing Cher and it made her feel like her little firecracker had turned into a softy for a second. "Cher, this my baby Troi." He introduced wrapping his hand around Troi's waist. The two women hugged and Cher noticed the way he stared at Troi. It almost shocked her.

"You done got my baby to settle down. We ain't letting you go." Cher joked to Troi making everyone in the room laugh. Cher's face fell flat as Rich entered the kitchen. He stopped in his tracks surprised that she'd come. He hadn't seen or spoken to Cher in months and the sight of her made him both happy and infuriated. It was obvious that he was battling with love and hate in one movement. The smiles on everyone's faces turned still. He'd dampened the mood without even trying.

Sonny grabbed Troi's hand bypassing his brother leading the way out. He was in a good mood and he and Rich hadn't been seeing eye to eye. Once again he was preventing smoke from happening during the holidays. It was Sonny's favorite time of the year. So much had changed with their family that he was happy that they were bringing in the new year the same. Cher's appearance had been a surprise but a damn good one. She restored the small sense of normalcy that Sonny had growing up.

Rich's eyes stayed glued to Cher's as hers stayed glued to his. Kill could feel the deadly tension in the room and he placed his hand on his brother's shoulder. "Everyone's here," he told Rich trying to get him out of the room. He patted Rich on the shoulder twice more and Rich finally turned towards the door.

He didn't have words for Cher in that minute. So many days he'd wished she'd come home and now that she did he wanted to wring her neck. If not for Missy, for his kids. He'd missed out on more than he'd ever had and the thought of them being there caused him to leave her standing in the kitchen.

Cher watched as Kaylin, Kill, and Rich left her alone and for the first time she felt like an outcast. Like she didn't belong. She thought about getting her kids and leaving but she knew there was no way that could happen. There would be a bloodbath before Rich allowed her to knowingly take his kids again. *At least Sonny happy to see me.* She thought to herself while taking a deep breath. She walked out the kitchen and instantly her mood was changed. The smiles on everyone's faces, even Rich's as he held their sons in his arms. She couldn't leave with them if she wanted to. Music played lightly in through the sound system as the chefs brought the food platters into the dining areas sitting them on the table.

The sight of Nitro with a cane confused Cher. She wanted to ask but it wasn't the time nor place.

As everyone sat down and ate, Cher stayed in her own bubble in her own world. She pictured her baby girl with her. She could feel her. While everyone else had someone Cher could feel Chas's spirit and she was content with it. She stayed in her own mind talking to Wynni occasionally but for the most part Chasity was her company. *I miss you baby girl.*

Although everyone seemed to be enjoying themselves Rich's eyes were locked in on Cher like a magnet. He was trying to make her uncomfortable but instead he was making everyone else. Sonny felt relief that Rich's wrath had been redirected to someone else other than him but it was obvious that Rich would probably kill Cher before the night was over. The hatred emanated off him. Sonny was unsure if Rich even realized it.

"Dinner was great. That new chef is a keeper." Kaylin threw a shot and Cher caught it while smirking. *This ho don't know I'll really kill her.*

"It was, but ya last chef was better." Cher stood up gathering the plates up from the table. Imani and Wynni stood up following her. "Ladies, let's get acquainted and let the men do what they do." Cher instructed as she walked off. Since Kaylin wanted to be petty she was gonna show her, her middle name was pettiest.

"Who invited her here?" Rich asked his brothers as he sat his sons on his laps. He hadn't seen them in so long that all he wanted to do was hug on them. He'd lost his daughter and his sons a few months later. He finally had his sons back but one piece was missing.

Kill shot two fingers into the air taking accountability. He could tell his brother had it out for Cher and if he'd known it was that bad he wouldn't have invited her.

"How long y'all been communicating?" Rich asked, locking eyes with his brother.

"We don't communicate. She reached out to me for help, and I helped her out and invited her." He told half the truth. Nitro and Sonny sat back uncomfortably. Rich's vibe had been the same since he entered the building; it hadn't wavered even a little bit and it worried them. They had never seen him so determined to hate like he was that minute. The only people he had love for were Enoch and Legend.

"Why didnt you tell me my wife called you?"

Kill chuckled shaking his head realizing that Rich was a time bomb waiting to explode. He needed a reason to he was fishing for one and Kill was over it. "Cause the last time we talked about her you said you would kill her if you ever saw her again. Invited her here so you could see your kids. Maybe even ya could possibly have a conversation. But nah. You said what you mean and we all see that shit. But it's too hot. So chill."

Rich's temple throbbed as he tightly hugged his boys. Kill was right. He was too focused on the hate he had for Cher and he needed to bask in the time he had with his sons. "Legendary man, you've been taking care of your brother?"

"Yea mon, Enoch is getting bad now. He fall onto the floor when he don't get his way. And he hit me and bite me."

Rich sat back amused at his oldest son telling on his youngest. "And what you do when he do that?"

"Me bite him and hit him back. Then he come hug me and kiss me afterwards." Everyone laughed as Enoch placed two fingers to Legend and pinched him. "Owww! You see." Legend fussed as he pinched his brother back.

"That's right, anything he do to you. You do it back to him so he see how it feels. When he see that it don't feel good he'll stop." Rich taught his son while glancing at Sonny.

"I know but I think he like the pain daddy because he never stop." Rich couldn't help but laugh. He missed this, conversations with his sons. Enoch was about to turn two and it was obvious the terrible part had begun already and Rich was missing out. The thought of missing out on any more of his children's life pained him. He needed a solution. The way he and Cher was, there was no way they could go back to trying to be a family. They were both scorned and Rich's pride was too big. In his mind Cher was the damn devil and he needed to send her back home.

***

"So tell me, how in the hell did you get my little bro to settle down." Cher was impressed with Troi, she was a bad bitch no doubt. She looked like she was just what Sonny needed. She was mature, her shoulder length locs and natural coke bottle shape made Cher nod in approval. She was the kind of woman Sonny needed in his life. "How did y'all even meet."

Troi blushed thinking of all her encounters with Sonny, he was something special to her. "I'm a bartender at the underground. Nitro introduced us." Cher smiled like a proud mom. Conversations she'd never have with Chas she was happy, she was able to have it with Troi. "Honestly I didn't think Sonny and I would get as far as we did because he was a little rude. Do y'all know this nigga ran my boyfriend off?" All the women laughed. Cher, Troi, Kaylin, and Imani were all sitting in the VIP room mingling amongst one another. Cher and Kaylin played their shade off until they finally had to face it.

"Well whatever you're doing, keep doing it. I haven't seen him smile this much in a while, it look good on him." Cher could tell that she was going to like Troi. In her peripheral vision she could see Kaylin mugging her like she was ready to pop off at any minute so she turned her attention to her.

"So Kaylin, how are you and Kill doing." Cher looked directly in Kaylin's eyes. It was obvious her presence alone had Kaylin on ten all over again.

"We're better than ever, you should know. Y'all talk every week right." A cheap shot at Cher that no one else caught on to. No one was supposed to know that Kill called Cher once a week. If Rich found out, there was no telling what he would do.

"Why wouldn't I talk to my brother-in-law every week." Taking a sip out the wine glass she was drinking out of, Cher eyes her basically telling her to shut the fuck up.

"Yeah, brother-in-law." Scuffing Kaylin turned her attention to Imani. She was getting tired of Cher's voice. She knew how to hit Cher where it hurt but she would do it gracefully.

"Tell us a little about you Imani. Let's get to know each other a little more. I mean we will be seeing each other a little more, unless somebody runs away again." Kaylin couldn't stop taking cheap shots at Cher. Cher was trying her hardest not to break the glass she was holding over Kaylin head. *This bitch don't understand that I'm a Vado for a reason. I'll kill this hoe and hide her were nobody will find her.*

"It's not much to tell. I'm just trying to help Nitro get back to himself."

"Why does he have a cane?" Cher asked intruding on their conversation.

"His baby mama got him shot and he's on his rode to recover. He overdoes it in physical therapy and sometimes I have to step in. His anger been getting the best of him and I gotta be there to let him know better days are coming." Troi lifted her glass to click it with Imani.

"Girl tell me about it." All the ladies laughed, and again Kaylin rolled her eyes at Cher.

"Um Kaylin, can I talk to you in private for a second." Kaylin rose out of her seat and followed Cher out the room. All the men's eyes were on them. Rich eyes connected with his wifes, he missed her more than anything but he hated that bitch so much. Kill was sweating bullets, only thing he could think was what the fuck was they doing and why was they alone.

"Hey baby. I'm about to step out and talk to Cher." Kaylin walked over and kissed Kill on the lips. She knew what she was doing. She dared Cher to act up so she could have her husband kill her right where her daughter had died. Everything in Cher was telling her to go upside Kaylin's head. After showing out, Kaylin and Cher finally made their way outside the building.

"Listen bitch." Cher took a breath to calm down. "I know you dont know me to fucking well but listen and listen good. Keep talking slick at the mouth and imma have yo body sliced up and buried eight feet deep."

"thank god cooking doesn't require math"

"Shut the fuck up, I'm talking. I know exactly what I'm talking about. Did you forget I'm the queen of this bitch, I'm Badrick Wife. I run all this. I will bury you eight feet, throw two feet of dirt on yo ass bury a dog and continue putting dirt on you. Bitch they will never find yo dead ass." Stepping face to face with Kaylin, Cher thought her words had made a difference but it didn't. Instead Kaylin shook her head and drank from her glass.

"If you Rich wife, then why the fuck are you trying so hard to get my man dick. Bitch stay the fuck away from Kill before I air all yo business out. Yeah I saw them text messages and bitch he mine. I would hate for Rich to find out his wife tryna bounce on his little brother's big ass dick." Kaylin smiled thinking about the night before when she rode Kill until the sun shined through the window. "And bitch it's big too, I bet you wish you knew what it felt like." Kaylin turned to walk back inside leaving Cher with her mouth wide open and madder then she originally was. "You might wanna come inside with me, it's kinda cold out here." Kaylin walked in the door and she winked at Kill, letting him know that their entire conversation was about him.

Two minutes after Kaylin walked in, Cher walked in to let everybody know that she was leaving. She couldn't be around Kaylin for too much longer. She was sick of that bitch.

"Rich, you can keep the kids tonight, they missed you."

"Wa yuh staying at tonight? Let mih walk yuh out." Ruch stood up to help his wife but she declined, she wasn't ready to have a conversation with him.

"Kill can you walk me out please?" Cher knew what she was doing, she knew Kaylin wouldn't start a scene in front of everybody. She was calling her bluff. Throwing Cher under the bus was throwing Kill under the bus and Rich wasn't too stable. There was no telling how he'd take it.

"Yeah come on." Rich sat back in his seat and watched his brother care after his wife. After too many minutes passed Rich walked to the door and saw Cher and Kill in a heated conversation. All of his brothers were moving different and all of this shit was about to come to an end.

Chapter 25

Sleep had become Nitro's enemy since he'd been shot. The thought of going to sleep and never waking up again made him keep his eyes open until they couldn't anymore. His life had almost been taken away from him too soon and the reason behind it ate at him. The DeLeon's had come back right after he'd seen Genie and every part of him knew she had something to do with it. Genie was like a beauty queen that had invisible horns. The devil's advocate. She'd tried to get his life taken from him and it didn't sit right with Nitro. As much as he tried to shrug it off he couldn't. She was his child's mother and he would have to deal with her until their child turned eighteen. So until then he had to communicate with her. *Coparent*, whatever that was. Nitro didn't know how the hell a DeLeon and a Vado had come together. He beat himself up about it everyday not understanding how he hadn't known. If he had, he would've killed her ass a long time ago and been on his merry little way. But instead he fucked with her and got burned each and every time. The thought of Genie beating him at his own game, time and time again ate at him.

He leaned over a sleeping Imani giving her a peck on the lips before he sat up in the bed. He grabbed his cane and threw on a pair of Nike sweats and a white tee placing a Nike hoodie over it. "Where you going?" Imani asked groggily in her sleep. After almost losing him she'd become a light sleeper. The entire time he'd been in a coma she'd listened closely to his heartbeat throughout her sleep to make sure that it didn't stop beating.

"I gotta go see that bitch." He told Imani honestly and instantly the sleep that filled her eyes disappeared as she sat up.

"I know you fucking kidding me right? For what? The bitch ain't try to kill your ass enough times. You still trying to see her?"

Nitro realized that Imani's insecurities were laid out on the surface. The fear of losing him to another woman still remained. He had no idea what walking away from her with Genie one time had done to her confidence. But she'd stuck around because she loved him and to hear him say that he was going to see Genie after all they'd been through he sounded like a clown.

"It's not like that ma. Shit was dead an over with. And she almost took my life because we together. What's stopping her from doing that shit again? This my life we talking about. For some gang shit my life already on the line. But some petty shit, my life ain't up for grabs." Nitro expressed as he took a seat at the edge of the bed. Since he'd been up he'd been in his head not letting anyone in. His near death experience had him shook, because it was proof that the power of a woman scorn was impeccable. Genie had come after him once and her coming after him a second time wasn't an option. Even if she was carrying his child.

"Well let's go," Imani told him while climbing out the bed. Nitro shook his head standing up.

"The two of yall in the same vicinity is a explosion ready to happen. The last time she put a hit out on a nigga. Just trust your man, ma."

Imani stood still with a frown on her face and panic in her heart and Nitro closed the gap between them. He slowly lifted her chin up and kissed her softly, his tongue separated her lips and their tongues danced around one another. It was a kiss of passion doing more reassuring than any of his words could do. Imani could feel herself about to melt in his arms and she placed both her hands flat onto his chest. "I trust you."

Although the words had come from her mouth, a part of her was nervous that if he walked through them doors he wouldn't re-enter. It could be from a bullet, or possibly because he chose Genie. But with all that he and Imani had been through she hoped like hell he wouldn't disappoint her. Because it would be the end. The last straw that would make her walk away.

"I'll be back before you wake up, get some rest."

A tightness filled Nitro's chest as he drove towards the DeLeon's estate. The closer he got the more angry he was. *This bitch put a hit out on me. I should shoot her between her eyes.* Nitro turned the thirty minute drive into a fifteen and when he finally made it to her house he parked the car. He sat behind the wheel for a few minutes as he realized that Genie was taking him out of character. The evil thoughts that invaded his mind made it easier to carry out the task. *She's pregnant with my kid.* He told himself to bring his smoke down. He couldn't allow his anger to get the best of him. Not with Genie. He pulled his 9mm out his waist and sat it in his lap just in case. With Genesis you could never be too careful. *Bitch move like a thief in the night.* He shot Genie a text and two minutes later the gates to the estate were opening.

Genie waltz down dressed in a Nike tech sweatsuit and a .45 in her hand. Her protruded 7 month belly led the way and Nitro rubbed his head as he shook it from side to side. *What the fuck did I do?* A full blown internal battle was in full effect and as Genie neared, Nitro blew out a breath climbing out his car. Cane in one hand, gun in the other.

Toxic, like ammonia and bleach, Genie and Nitro stood face to face grilling one another. Both of them with hate in their heart for the other, and wanting to pull the trigger but the baby they'd created halted them. Making them think of every decision they made towards one another and how it affected it.

"Why the fuck are you here?" Genie hissed. Nitro stared at her silently. Not talking until he felt like talking. He'd realized that Genie thought she ran the show because he'd let her. But every bit of love he'd had for her had gone out the window the day he'd been shot. So instead he stared. His eyes ran from her head to her feet making her uncomfortable. So uncomfortable her nerves were bad and her hand shook. She slowly walked up to him, closing the gap. Being uncomfortable was no longer an option. Because her adrenaline ran and her heart hurt along with her ego.

"You set me up G?" Nitro asked, still unable to process her treachery. He couldn't believe that he'd been played by a bitch and the reality of it pained him.

"Your brothers killed my father, so let's just drop it. We're even." Nitro looked at her like he'd heard her wrong. His brows creased together and he turned his lip up at her. The way the words had come from her mouth so casually like everything was resolved baffled him.

"We not even G, you sent for me when you didn't have to. You almost took me out cause your jealousy. You mad about a spot you never had and that shit blinded you. Did you think about the baby then? Cause since I found out all I think about is the baby. The baby the only person saving me from putting a fucking bullet in you ma."

Nitro's words were like a knife through Genie's already broken heart. Her actions had come back around full circle. She'd lost her protector and everyday she'd tried taking her own life. But his words were true. Their baby was the only thing that kept her alive. She was alive but was barely living. His words had gutted her. Pushed her over the edge. She placed the gun to her head as tears ran from her eyes. Her finger was on the trigger ready. Her eyes were telling him sorry because she was about to wreck both of their worlds.

Every part of Nitro wanted her to pull the trigger except the part that had already mentally prepared to have a kid. Life was short and him nearly dying and coming back to life made him ready. He'd held his son, embraced him, played with him and put him . Risked the little bit of life that God held onto him by to be a father.

"Genesis," He swiftly pulled her into him as a bullet shot through the gun

BANG!

Nitro's heart beat wildly in his chest. He let his cane go slightly, losing his balance as he held her into his arms. The car held them up for support and he ran his hand over her hair and he pulled the gun from her hand. "No G, what are you doing ma?"

Genie finally cried into his chest finally feeling like a part of him had softened up. She needed someone to be soft with her. Everyone else had shunned her out their lives. Everyday guilt was eating at her and she hadn't pulled a trigger because she knew no one would care. But Nitro would. No matter how much he hated her.

As long as his baby was in her belly he would protect her. She saw it in his eye. The look a good father had in their eye when they spoke on their children was noticed. She saw her father in Nitro and he'd proven he would be the best.

He wrapped his arms around her holding onto her as he placed his head back onto the window letting out a deep breath. Genie could hear his heart racing. It was racing at the same speed as hers. Tears dropped from her eye like rain as a wail escaped her lips. She regretted ever meeting him. Because she loved him so much. No matter how much she hated him the love outweighed it. She'd fallen for the enemy and he'd turned her crazy.

"I can't do this without you, I just can't." Genie cried as she held onto his sweater. She listened to his heart rate as it sped faster and faster. The faster it raced the harder she cried. He'd broken her and he would fix her. Without a choice. A life without Nitro wasn't a life she was willing to live. The only other man she loved the way she loved Nitro was gone. By the hands of his family. The only person she had to live for was in her belly and she knew Nitro would make sure she lived.

***

"How much longer until you get here, I found the movies that we can watch tonight." Kaylin sat back on her couch while facetiming Kill. They were about to watch a couple movies and chill. Enjoy one another company like they'd been doing. Everything was sweet in their household because as always Kill was treating his pregnant girlfriend like a queen. Movies weren't on his agenda for the day but when Kay called Kill answered and obliged. If they were going to have a baby he needed everything to be perfect.

After going to a few appointments and being notified of Kaylin's stress levels, Kill didn't add to it.

"I'll be there in like an hour ma, I'm finishing up some stuff with my bros and I'm on my way to you."

"Okay get here safe. We love you." Kaylin smiled into the phone.

"I love y'all too." Kaylin hung up her phone and began to rub her stomach. This was the life that she had always imagined herself living. A life with Akiel was what she wanted.

Kaylin turned the tv to her favorite show All American and watched it until sleep consumed her.

"Let's hurry up and find this bitch, make sure you have yo gloves on, we don't need nothing coming back to us."

Kaylin shot up when she heard the voices in her subconscious state. *There's somebody here.* Her heart raced as her fight or flight senses kicked in. The thought of two against her and her baby caused her to tip toe to her room, which was only a few feet from her living room. She rushed into her master bedroom locking the door and grabbing the gun that she kept in her nightstand. Kaylin crept into the master bathroom pulling the curtain back as she laid down in the tub.

"Oh my God I forgot my phone in the living room." She whispered to herself. Her heart raced and she closed her eyes saying a quick prayer. *God please help me and my baby. Make Akiel walk through them doors. Please just help me.*

"Where the fuck is this bitch at?" Kaylin heard one of the intruders in her bedroom pulling out drawers, slamming doors, breaking things. The female voice threw her off. *There's a bitch in there.*

"Aye go check behind that door right there." She heard a man's voice give directions. Kaylin covered her mouth and whimpered, as she heard the knob twisting. This wasn't the way she wanted to die.

"Shoot the fucking knob off, I bet that bitch in there. I have her phone right here and her car parked outside." One of the men yelled. Kaylin stepped out of the bathtub and prepared herself to try to run out the door. She aimed at the door sending the first shot through it. She ducked off to the side as bullets rained down on her bathroom door. Kaylin shot back knowing that she couldn't go down without a fight.

She stopped shooting to preserve the last few bullets she had. She watched as a masked man stepped through the door and let a shot go into his leg. Another masked man rushed over to her tackling her causing her gun to drop.

"Get the fuck off of me! My baby. Oh my God my baby." Kaylin cried as his heavy set frame pinned her down by the throat. She could feel the little bit of air in her lungs leaving.

"Shut the fuck up, before I knock yo ass out." Kaylin struggled against him getting weaker and weaker as she kicked her legs and her arms flew freely. She clawed until she couldn't anyone, the pressure on her throat had her seeing stars and she was getting dizzy. She could feel herself about to die, and her heart felt like it would explode.

"Please, please, my baby." Kaylin whispered in between breaths as she stopped fighting and placed her hand on her stomach. The masked man choked her until she was and limp. Picking her up, he laughed at his partner on the floor.

"Get yo ass up, how you get shot by a bitch." Getting off the floor the second masked man limped after his partner.

"Let's see if Kill loves her enough to find her before I bury her ass alive. They played with the wrong bitch." The woman seated on the couch chuckled as she walked out of the house in her six inch heels with a smile on her face. She led them to her truck and open the back door as they threw Kaylin in the back like a rag doll and drove off.

When Kill finally made it to Kaylin's house he immediately knew something was wrong. Kaylin's front door was wide open. He hopped out the car and parked his car. Kill pulled his gun off his hip and walked over to the door.

"Kaylin!" he called out as he entered her house. His gun was aimed as he waited to see if he'd hear something. But when he saw the TV smashed, sofas slashed and glass everywhere he rushed into the bedroom. The traces of blood drove Kill crazy and he was livid.

Killa Kay. "Ma where the fuck you at." He whispered as he thought out loud. He was thinking about who would've come after her. *DeLeons?* Kill was trying to get his mind to point out any possible threat to him and the DeLeons were at the top of the list. He hoped it was then so he could finish off what Sonny started. Either way somebody had his girl and he was about to paint Georgia red until he found her. Kill was tired of people trying the Vado family, it was time to remind them why they called him Kill. Cause everyone was dead from this disrespect.

As he walked towards the front door Kill stopped in his tracks. *My baby*. It had been the first time Kill acknowledged the baby that Kaylin was carrying. His emotions got the best of him, he realized that he did love this baby and he wanted this baby. Walking out the door and locking it, Kill called Nitro and told him to meet him at Rich house. Kill was ready for War.

Chapter 26

Walking through the doors at Rich house Sonny, headed straight into the living room where he heard the TV playing at.

"What's up bro, you wanted to talk to me." Sonny slapped hands with his brother as he took a seat across from him.

"Ya mih did. Mih gon get strait to di point. Let mih be yuh partner, wi can both run dis business." Rich wasn't asking. He was demanding. Pulling his age rank to try to get Sonny back under his wing. Still thinking Sonny was still the little nigga who diapers he used to change. He was trying to swindle Sonny into letting him run the business. Because in Rich's mind Sonny was still his son.

"I'm good bro, I got so much shit planned for this. You know how long I been waiting on thid position. I used to talk to you about running the business" Sonny cracked open the beer that was sitting in front of him taking a gulp.

"Bro, yuh only twenty-one, yuh don't need any responsibility like dis. Let's tawk tuh unc and tell him yuh no want it."

"Don't want it. What the fuck are you talking about? Why I don't want it? This is all I ever wanted." Sonny barked, losing patience. It was something about his oldest brother that got under his skin so easily. Rich had no regard for Sonny and his age. The look of disgust on Rich's face caused him to continue. "Don't tell me you mad at me for accepting this position." Sonny scoffed as he placed the beer onto the table and headed towards the door.

"Yuh know this mih fucking business. Mih run dis shit not yuh. Either yuh handing it over or mih taking it from yuh." Sonny stopped in his tracks and walked back towards his big brother. The nigga who used to be his role model, the nigga who raised him.

"Is that a threat Rich, I don't take too kindly to them and you know that." Rich stood up and stood toe to toe with his little brother. Seeing that Rich wasn't playing and his threat was solid Sonny lost it. The part of him that Troi had worked so hard for him not to be.

"WELL TAKE IT FROM ME BRO!" Sonny barked in his face. He wasn't backing down for nothing. He was tired of being guilted, he was tired of being ashamed and he was tired of being sonned.

"If it wasn't for yuh, wi wouldn't have been in tis mess. Yuh the cause of all dis beef and yuh tink yuh can run dis business. Di only place yuh wi run it, is to the ground." Rich was pressing Sonny's buttons.

"Well mih fix mih mistake! I killed Alejandro not yuh. Unc gave you plenty of opportunities to kill Alejandro and yo bitch ass couldn't even do that. Let me school you big bro, let me take you under my wing." Sonny taunted Rich. For the first time he could see Rich sweating. He was damn near foaming at the mouth. Sonny knew he was getting under his skin.Rich didn't take rejection from his younger siblings too well. "What's yo problem with me bro, I know it's more than just this damn business. Do what pops and unc taught us, speak yo fucking mind dont be silent."

"Yuh got mih daughter killed, if it wasn't for yuh, She would still be here. If yuh wasn't so hot headed da DeLeon's couldn't have come after us. Sonny yuh a fuck up baby brotha!" Rich yelled as he stepped in Sonny's face. His eyes were bulging and blood shot red. He was no longer seeing his baby brother. He was seeing an enemy. The one who caused the catalyst in his life. The person who had taken his throne from him. The smirk on Sonny's face sent a chill through Rich. It was official, his younger brother no longer respected him. He'd made peace with himself over his mistakes. But Rich would never have peace and he would allow Sonny to have any. He pulled his gun out and aimed it at his brother. "You killed my daughter! You killed a part of me Carson. And you're trying to take away my business but I can't let you." Rich shook his head from side to side as he stepped back keeping his aim steady. At the pull of a trigger the bullet would kill his baby brother. He would be doing them all a favor taking out the bad apple. And he would get his throne back. The idea of it all was enough to make Rich curl his finger over the trigger.

BANG BANG!

To Be Continued...

Note from Author's

Thank you all for your support. This is our first release of the year and we hope we fed your minds. We gave you an escape and we hope you enjoyed every minute of the rollercoaster with these brothers. Enough to come back for part two

Follow us on social media for update on VADO: Violence and Drugs Only 2

Instagram: theofficialbookfairy

Facebook: Author DAK

Twitter: iamdak1

Instagram: author_tiffanys

Facebook: Author T. Marie

Twitter: AuthorTMarie

Acknowledgements

Oh yeaahhhhhh, one more motherfucking thang! Shoutout to the motherfucking mafia. I fuck with y'all heavy. Lmao staying up countless nights keeping me company with my edits, while I write, and just becoming a lil literary family. I love it here!

Join their Facebook group "Midnight Mafia & Tingz"

About Author DAK

I never know what to say in bio's because honestly there's no way to put it. You just have to see for yourself and depict your own image of me. The truest thing about Dak is imma mother before anything. My kids are my pocketbooks and broke besties. They come first forever and always. They've been my motivation on rough days and I have penned 18 books since becoming a mother. From signed to self publish and I'm not doing too shabby if I might say so myself. I'm coming for the orange banner on Amazon. That #1 best selling spot, after that New York Times here I come. Your girl got some more heat cooking up and there's no stopping me.

About Author T. Marie

T.Marie formally known as Author Tiffany Singleton was born and raised in Flint MI. She was signed to True Glory Publications from years 2017-2020 and recently went Indie the summer of 2020! Writing became her passion when her GodFather died when she was in the 8th grade! Starting with Poetry, she released a book with over 25 poems in it all related to love, death, and life. She moved to urban fiction when she realized how passionate writing was to her and how it kept her at peace! Writing is the only thing that keeps her head on right! When her dad died in 2018, she wanted to give it all up but she kept thriving and that same year she became a best selling Author! Her word to you: Never give up on your dreams; Better times are coming!

Made in the USA
Monee, IL
26 March 2021